Working Backwards from
the Worst Moment of My Life

Working Backwards from the Worst Moment of My Life

stories by

Rob Roberge

 RED HEN PRESS | *Pasadena, CA*

Book layout by Elizabeth Davis
Book design by Mark E. Cull

Roberge, Rob.
    Working backwards from the worst moment of my life / Rob
Roberge.—1st ed.
    p. cm.
  ISBN 978-1-59709-165-7
  I. Title.
  PS3618.O31525W67 2010
  813'.6—dc22

                        2010026684

The Annenberg Foundation, the James Irvine Foundation, the Los
Angeles County Arts Commission, and the National Endowment for
the Arts partially support Red Hen Press.

First Edition

Published by Red Hen Press
Pasdena, CA
www.redhen.org

Acknowledgements

"Working Backwards from the Worst Moment of My Life" appeared in *Chelsea/59*. "The Exterminator" in *Another City: Writing From Los Angeles* (City Lights Books) & *It's All Good* (Manic D Press); "Love & Hope & Sex & Dreams" and "Beano's Deal" in *Other Voices;* "Swiss Engineering" in *Zzyyva;* "Burn Ward" (as "Live Audiences") in *Alaska Quarterly Review*; "Border Radio" in *Santi: Lives of Modern Saints* (Black Arrow Books); "Earthquake" in *Parting Gifts;* "Whatever Happened to Billy Brody?" in *Vortical Magazine;* "A Headache from Barstow to Salt Lake" in *Zink: A LitZine;* "Do Not Concern Yourself with Things Lee Nading Has Left Out" in *The Literary Review*.

Special thanks to, in no particular order:

The fabulous Kate Gale, Mark Cull and everyone at Red Hen—if there's a better press to work with, they're keeping it a good secret.

Michael Kimball for his generous and intelligent editorial notes. Francois and Spence for their friendship all these years and for teaching me how to write. My agent and friend Gary Morris for standing by me and my work all these years. Tod Goldberg for his generosity and wit and all-around greatness. Gina Frangello, for her support with this book and for her own great writing. Katie Arnoldi, great friend and writer. Steve Wynn for being a great guy and being one of the main contributors of the soundtrack of my life. To my wonderful family. Mike Martt, fabulous friend and amazing songwriter, for letting me read large pieces of this at the Writer's Garage. Christine @ Smartgals.org, for so many reasons. Steve Almond for his friendship, writing and all-around chocolaty goodness. Orlando Cartaya for fixing my brain and being an amazing friend. Mike Robinson, for the guitars, the humor and the friendship. My students at Antioch and at UCLA Extension, for keeping me sharp and for teaching me so much, along with letting me teach you. Steve Heller & Tara Ison (at Antioch) and Linda Venus (at UCLA Extension), for letting me teach in your great programs. Kev Cain, super friend and one of the funniest people on the planet. And to all my great band mates—I love you all, you noisy bastards.

In alphabetical order—Antonia, Billy, Gayle, Mike M and Patrick for helping keep me clean and keeping my head out of the oven in this world that to me seems at times pretty oven-laden.

And to all my friends—who make life worth living and who are, lucky me, too numerous to list here. Thank you.

Contents

This book is for, and largely because of, Gayle. Without you, I'd be lost beyond words. Love, always, to you, who makes everything around you more beautiful. You rock in so many ways, Bud.

Working Backwards from
the Worst Moment of My Life

Working Backwards from the Worst Moment of My Life

I

At this moment, Tommy Cronin, whose mental capacity has been professionally measured at equal to that of a three year old is being pelted with raw eggs by me and his father who everyone except Tommy calls Pops. Tommy's one of those carnival ducks at a shooting gallery; every time he's hit, he turns and marches the other way. The misses, the eggs and garbage, they smack and drip on the wall behind him.

Me and Pops hit him one after the other and he turns all jerky back and forth. This would be Keystone Cops, this would be Fatty Arbuckle, if it weren't in color and it weren't real.

And this is Pops' punishment. Not Pops' punishment to Tommy, but to me. This is my penance.

II

Understand that I've known Pops my whole life and I owe him too much to recount.

To Pops, I'm Smart Guy. I can't remember when he first called me that, but it stuck. I grew up with Tommy, played on Pop Warner and Babe Ruth teams that Pops coached. I started working at Pops' religious memorabilia factory underage at fourteen.

My first two summers, I made Christs. To be more accurate, I inspected plastic Christs at their last stop before being packed and shipped. Inspection was the end of the line and not much could go wrong. The two trouble spots were the paint and the mold joints where Christ and the cross met.

The cross had three holes where the nails would've gone. A machine clicked them together. Sometimes, when the mold operator set the timers off, the holes would fill with plastic and Christ would be improperly fastened. Down the line, you'd see them coming. Christ dangling off his cross, arms unstuck, looking like a diver at the moment of dismount. My job was to toss them in a box for meltdown so they could be re-done.

After two years of that, Pops put me copy editing on Bibles. We did old and new Testaments, plus the Book of Mormon and what I was told was a shoddy translation of the Koran. Since the early ''50s, he'd had the Holiday Inn contract and it was strict company policy to stay at Holiday Inn's on your vacation and steal their Bibles. Every stolen Bible was money in Pops' pocket. You came back from vacation and you presented Pops with your stolen Bibles. You didn't, his potential royalty came out of your pocket.

"You don't steal for Pops, you're stealing from Pops."

A world view. Not open to debate.

III

A year ago, Pops' only son Tommy shot himself through the right temple. The bullet exploded the left side of his head—crushed and pushed the wall of his skull out like a burst dam—exited and came to rest in the wall. The best doctors Pops could buy, which is to say the best anyone could buy, re-built the left side of his head as well as they could, but it's still caved in like a rotting orange. Tommy pretty much lobotomized himself; he walks through life like some horror-movie zombie. Every couple months, they have to drain fluid from what's left of his brain.

IV

I was out in Los Angeles, trying to get some work in the movies when this happened. Pops called and asked me to come back and help out and I did. I owe Pops big. He sent me to college—undergrad and film school—and gave me twenty grand to get started out West. Plus, Pops asking and Pops demanding is a distinction without a difference and I've met very few people who could afford to get on his bad side.

For about six months, Pops played the role of dutiful father—helped Tommy rehab his atrophied body and ignored the doctors who said there was no hope for mental rehab. For the first month, Tommy was still pretty touch and go, too deep a sleep could potentially slip him into a coma. Me and Pops stayed up with him, slept at one hour intervals and shook Tommy gently at the top of every hour.

The cops took the slug out of the wall and I ended up wiping down the wall of blood and brain and bone and patching the hole. The carpet was replaced.

After six months of day-to-day care, Tommy finally spoke. He looked at Pops, eyes all distant. "Dad?" he said.

No one, except the DA, has ever called Pops anything but Pops. "Dad?" Tommy said again. Pops left the room. And this bubbled-eyed relic of Tommy looks up at me.

"Yeah," I say. "That's your dad."

And Tommy nodded, his eyes drifting.

I wasn't used to his eyes yet. They vibrate, his eyes do, like those lottery ping-pong balls the second before they get sucked up the tube. Bouncy and weightless. Like there was nothing, absolutely nothing, in front of or behind them.

A little after Tommy began talking, the doctors confirmed Pops' fear. Along with little detectable emotion, Tommy has no memory. After this, Pops hired 24-hour care for Tommy and spent next to no time with him.

What Tommy is now, as far as he knows, he has always been.

V

Pops asked me to stay in town instead of going back to California.

"Sure," I said. "How long?"

"Until this is resolved."

And I thought, but didn't say: Resolved? The way things are now with Tommy are the way they'll always be. What Pops had in mind, I didn't ask. Maybe I would have left if I'd known, but I doubt it.

VI

Me and Pops are out on his deck. He's drinking Jack Daniels and I've got a Bass Ale. This is a few months ago.

"Let's say you have a child," he says. "Hypothetical."

I nod. "I have a hypothetical child," I say.

"No jokes, Smart Guy."

He looks at me and I put both hands up. I'm that mime in a box. Message received. Pops is on one of his philosophical drunks and this is a serious talk.

"OK. I have a child."

"Good. And it's a hermaphrodite."

"Hermaphrodite?"

"Hermaphrodite, shit for brains. You don't know what that is?"

And we're on the verge of Philosophical Pops turning into Violent Pops, so I just nod.

"Anyway," he says. "There is no dominant sexual trait. The doctors tell you this." Pops lights two cigarettes and gives me one. "You with me?"

"So far."

"And the doctor gives you the choice and it's your choice alone. What do you make that kid? A boy or a girl?"

"There's no dominant trait?" I say.

Pops shakes his head. "None."

"And I'm alone in the decision?"

"For the sake of this conversation, yes."

I take a sip of my beer. Some kids are lighting firecrackers out in the street.

"I have no idea," I say. "I think I'd leave it as is."

"You can't," Pops says.

"I can too," I say. "There's no law that says I couldn't."

"You want a bet," Pops says. "You can't leave a kid like that. Not in this world. You have to make a choice."

And it hits me. "We're not talking hypothetically?" I say.

"No." Pops pours himself another drink. "You're the first—other than his mother—and the last that knows this. Are we clear on that, Smart Guy?"

And I nod that, yes, we are clear on that.

"Your problem," he tells me, "is that you can't stand up and make a decision. Even a fucking hypothetical one, for Christ's sake." He takes a drink. "But you're going to have to now."

"What?"

"I love you like a son," he says.

And I'm worried now that we're headed into drunken Sentimental Pops, but I'm way off.

"I want you to kill him," he says.

This is one of those moments in life where you're talking just to hear the words. Like they'll make more sense out of your mouth, you know?

"Kill him?" I say.

"I fucked that kid up. This is guilt I'm talking about, Smart Guy. Pay attention. This is a life lesson you're getting for free. I fucked that kid up in a way most men could never begin to comprehend. I'm not talking I didn't spend enough time with him, or I worked too late at the office, or I wasn't discreet enough when I screwed the secretaries, I talking big time—capital B, capital T—mistake."

He takes a tumbler of whiskey in one shot and pours another.

"That's on my head. Whatever the fuck led Tommy to put that gun to his head, I started in motion. My fault. Forever. Whatever made him too fucking dumb to use a nine millimeter instead of a twenty-two or pills, that's his fault. But he wanted to die and I've tried and I can't do it. He's still mine."

"Pops," I say. "What you're asking."

"I'm not asking. Decision time, Smart Guy. If he lives like this, now it's your fault."

VII

My first year in film school, we had to do a documentary about our summer break. Mine was about Pops and the factory. It's a shitty film. I had very little idea how to make one, and documentary is a tough form. You think the material is all there and all you have to do is shoot it and edit it and that's where it gets tricky.

What do you cut out of life to make it seem lifelike?

Since that night on Pops' porch, I've watched that film more times than I can count. I've looked at Tommy in stop-frame and tried to spot signs of unhappiness. Signs of confusion. And they're there, but they're not.

There's an interview with Pops. He's at his desk and behind him are two of the company's sayings:

THE WORD OF POPS IS THE WORD OF THE LORD

and:

DON'T FORGET TO STEAL THEIR BIBLES

Pops is in good spirits. On the day I filmed, he was as proud of me as he'd ever been up to that point. He got drunk that night and turned into Sentimental Pops.

"If I had ten sons," he said. "I'd want them all to turn out like you."

I felt a little uneasy. "What about Tommy?"

"Tommy's different," he said. And again, looking back, it makes more—or different—sense than it did.

But on film, before he got drunk that night, he's Proud Pops, strutting around his factory wearing a pin stripe suit that makes him look like a middle-aged gangster, showing off machinery, and sitting behind a desk that would make a President blush.

"The problem with your generation, Smart Guy" he said to me and the camera, "is that you haven't had enough wars. No war. No depression. You're soft."

Later in the film, I asked him if he was religious.

"No," he said.

"Then why this business?"

"I sold home security when I was your age. This is before electronics and all that shit. We were selling people, a service, understand. Neighborhood Security Guards I guess would be what they were. We'd call people and ask if they wanted a neighborhood patrol. If they said no, we'd hire kids to throw brick through their windows. They'd want security then. I got caught. So I got into religious memorabilia." And here, on the tape, he shrugs. "It's legit. No institutional peckerheads to deal with except the I.R.S."

As I said, it was a terrible film. Among other things, the editing was poor since I never got it past Rough Cut, but Pops came off very well. The class loved him.

I watch this film and see how proud he is, think of how much I owe this man and the only way to give him some peace makes me sick. And now, it's stuck on me. Right or wrong, Tommy, with his dead, bouncy stare and caved-in head is now my fault. He's been passed to me.

VIII

Pops doesn't talk to me for a while, says he's waiting for me to "make the first real decision of my life" and I think of heading back West, but I can't.

Then, earlier tonight, he calls and invites me to dinner. Sounds like he's in a great mood, like nothing has come between us. Like we've never talked about me killing his son and my friend.

I get to the house and he meets me at the door with Tommy. His eyes lull and roll and there's drool milky-white on his lips.

"We're taking Rain Man with us, OK Smart Guy?"

I don't say a word in the car. Tommy keeps saying "Dad? Where we goin'?" over and over. Every time, Pops points at me.

"Ask him, Tommy" Pops says. "Ask Smart Guy."

So Tommy alternates between:

"Dad? Where we goin'?"

and

"Smart Guy? Where we goin'?"

His voice is hollow, slow and drawn out like a hopeless dog at the pound. His head rocks more than a normal person's, like either it weighs more, or the neck's no good.

Finally, I say, "I don't know, Tommy."

At the restaurant, Pops charms the hostess and gets us a table by the window. The waiter and the busser come to the table and they both do a double-take on Tommy. They look away quickly.

"No," Pops says to them. "Go ahead, look." He tells Tommy to stand up. He does. "Everybody," Pops screams. "Look over here." He pokes at Tommy and tells him to walk to the door and come back.

And Tommy does as he's told. Pops tells him to do it again. And he does. When he walks from our table for the third time, Pops stands on his chair and yells.

"That's my son! Him there with half a head and half a fucking brain to match with the goo-goo-googily eyes." Pops is a carney barker and Tommy's his geek show. "Step right up and see the freak! He's mine, folks! You all getting a good look? Look deep in his eyes. Might as well stare at a fucking shoebox. That's my son!"

Tommy turns and starts to come back to the table. Pops grabs me hard at the back of my neck and points my head toward Tommy.

"You getting a good look, Smart Guy?" He releases me hard. I rub the back of my neck and look down at the table. Pops pokes me in the shoulder with a finger stiff as rebar a couple of times before I look up.

"Smart Guy," Pops says. He's crying. "That's your brother. That sad, pathetic freak is your brother. Get used to this."

IX

We get back to the house and Pops sends the nurse home. The three of us, me Tommy, and Pops, go down to the family room. Pops tells me to sit on the couch; he places Tommy by the far wall and tells him to stay. He comes back to the living room with a box full of egg cartons.

"Two choices," Pops says. "One, you and me, we throw these eggs at him. Parade him back and forth and throw this shit at him. Two, you do right thing and kill him."

"I can't."

"You won't," Pops says. "There's a difference."

"We're talking about Tommy," I say.

"No more talk. You're going to have to choose. It's treat him like the sad freak that he is, or end what should already be over. One or the other."

Pops throws the first egg.

"Tommy," I say.

"Tommy's dead and that thing in front of you can't remember its name," Pops says. "Make a decision."

I could kill myself right now. People say that—I've said that—but now, I think I could. I've never wanted to be farther away from where I am than at this moment.

I throw an egg that hits Tommy in the shoulder and breaks.

"You're chickenshit," Pops says to me. "I love you, but you're chickenshit. I asked you a favor. One fucking favor." Then Pops talks to Tommy. "We're going to play a game now," Pops says and Tommy nods. "Turn around and walk the other way whenever you get hit, OK?"

"OK, Dad," Tommy says.

Pops turns to me. "I'm trying to teach you something here, Smart Guy. You're all that's left."

And now, Tommy Cronin is being pelted with raw eggs by me and Pops. I'm crying, sobbing, and it's one of those child-like ones that I can't turn off. Pops hits Tommy with an egg; Tommy turns around. Tommy turns around; I hit him with an egg. And my brain right now is a tape-loop of I could-haves and I should-haves.

And nothing prepared me for this. If there was a role I should have played, I didn't know it. Pop throws an egg. I throw an egg. Tommy turns around.

A train leaves New York at 75 miles per hour. Another train leaves Los Angeles at 60 miles per hour. The New York train stops every four hours to unload; the Los Angeles train goes non-stop. Where do they meet?

And you don't know so you guess. You guess somewhere in the middle. You look at the map, point dead center, and you guess a couple hundred miles one way or the other. You have no idea how to arrive at the correct answer.

Pops left out a third option. I could leave and never come back. Hit the West Coast and try to block this, store it away. But I can't. Or won't. Pops is doing what he's done my whole life; he's playing the percentages and the odds are always with the house. He knows that and I know that.

"You're missing on purpose," Pops says.

I throw another and Tommy turns around.

The Exterminator

The exterminator drives a canary-yellow company van with enormous mouse ears on top and a fake mouse nose painted on the spare tire mounted on the grille. Across the side of the van is the company phone number and the logo, "We're The Critter Ridders."

He comes to a white farmhouse with an old amateur stone wall bordering the road and driveway. The farmhouse is on the crest of a hill and it has a crumbling Norman Rockwell porch. The porch is in a terrible state of neglect, tilted and falling into the ground. It looks like a wheelchair ramp with a love seat, grown over with weeds.

The exterminator walks to the door. A couple in their mid-twenties, about his age, meet him.

"We've got a rat trapped in the bathroom," the man says.

"Yeach," the exterminator says. "I hate rats."

"You hate rats?" the man says. He looks at the exterminator, then at the woman, wide-eyed in disbelief.

The exterminator shrugs. "It's a job, right?" He walks past where they are in the entrance of the kitchen. "Bathroom?" he says.

They lead him out of the kitchen, into a room full of heavy-looking Victorian furniture and into a living area. The man points to a closed door.

"He's in there?" the exterminator says.

"It's in there," the man says.

The exterminator puts his ear to the door. "Male," he says.

"How can you tell?" the man says.

"Females never get trapped. Too smart."

"Really?" the woman says.

"Really," the exterminator says, although he actually has no clue to the sex of the vermin. The exterminator makes things up. He's told clients that roaches, as far as entomology can determine, have sex for fun as well as procreation, that fleas mate for life—albeit a short life, and that mice bite their finger and toenails to keep them sharp.

He has no idea whether any of this is true.

The exterminator walks away from the bathroom. His boots clump on the hardwood floor. He tells the couple he'll be back in a moment with the tools he'll need.

Snow is falling. The exterminator feels as if time were standing still. He will open the back of the company van in a moment. He's in the company-issue uniform; thick steel-toed boots and a canary yellow jumpsuit with a beeper hooked into the belt.

The exterminator:

Bites his nails.

Suffers from insomnia.

Hates driving a van that's made to look like a giant rodent.

Has not always been an exterminator.

Has a daughter he's never seen.

Can't stand to be alone.

Is not fond of others.

Has a Beagle named Fausto.

Smokes two packs of cigarettes a day.

Goes to AA meetings sometimes.

Knows a man who glazes hams for a living, a man he used to drink with.

Misses drinking more than the daughter.

Is not bothered by not seeing his daughter.

Is bothered that it doesn't bother him.

Is standing in snowfall.

He opens the back of the van and the overhead light comes on. He takes out four long boxes and leans them on the bumper. He thinks of using traps and quickly decides against them.

The last time he used traps, he splattered the walls of a house with blood and had to stay behind, off the clock, to clean.

He takes a rubber mallet from the van, gathers the four boxes and kicks the door closed. It doesn't close properly and the light is left on. He walks back to the house.

At the door to the bathroom, the exterminator bends down and opens the first of the four boxes, which are about a yard long. He handles the glue sticks with gloves, peeling back the protective layer.

The glue sticks look like ordinary baseboard but, once peeled, are incredibly sticky. Guaranteed to hold a twenty pound rodent helpless. The exterminator hopes never to test this promise. He looks up at the man.

"You got a big shovel?"

"A shovel?"

The exterminator nods. "A big one."

"Why?"

"Because I'm going to try and trap him with glue sticks, but he might get away. I need to open the door so he thinks he can escape. That's when—if he's not stuck—you lower the shovel on him."

"What are we paying you for?" the woman says.

The exterminator gets out of his catcher's stance and stands up. "Look," he says. "I can cover the walls in there so ugly that you'll spend the next six months finding little rat parts on everything. This way is much neater."

The exterminator feels guilty for snapping at the woman, as he always does when he says what he's really thinking. He smiles an apologetic smile. "I'm sorry," he says. "Trust me."

"Fine," she says. "Just get it out of here."

"I've got a snow shovel," the man says.

"Good," the exterminator says. The man starts out of the room. "And put on some boots if you've got 'em."

"Boots?" The man looks worried.

"Boots. Thick." He finishes opening the boxes of glue strips.

The man comes down the stairs, wearing boots, carting a shovel, a tennis racket and another pair of boots. "Here," he says to the woman, handing her the boots and tennis racket.

"In case he gets by me," the man says.

"He probably won't even get out of the bathroom," the exterminator says.

"Just in case," the man says. The woman puts on the boots and stands behind the man, holding the tennis racket.

"I'm going in," the exterminator says. "You ready?"

The man nods and the exterminator realizes that he's actually getting into this. "Ready," he says.

The exterminator opens the door and immediately sees the rat run under the large claw-foot bathtub. He lays the glue strips, one on each wall in front of the floor boards. The side with less adhesive sits toward the wall. The other, much stickier side, faces out to trap the rat.

He gets in the tub, mallet in hand, and starts jumping up and down, trying to scare the rat out of hiding.

"OK. Open the door," he says.

On the third jump, he catches his reflection in the mirror, a great yellow flash going up and down. His boots are dirtying the tub.

The exterminator senses the couple beginning to doubt him.

"Done it a thousand times," he lies. "Best method."

On the tenth or eleventh jump, the rat runs to the middle of the bathroom. It looks one way then another. The man moves the shovel and the rat runs away from it, straight into a glue stick. Its two right legs are stuck to the board, the other two scrape against the black and while tiled floor making a high-pitched noise.

The exterminator gets out of the tub. "You might want to close the door now," he says. The man leaves the door open.

The exterminator brings the mallet down on the rat's skull. It makes the same crunching noise his boots made on the frozen ground. The rat rolls away from the blow and is now stuck full on its back. It lets out a moan that sounds almost human, a noise too big for such a small creature. The second hit ends it. Dark blood, the color of aged mahogany, trickles onto the glue strip.

The exterminator puts on gloves and takes the rat out to the van. He scrapes it, using the mallet, into a destruction box that he will take to the office destruction wing. The used glue strip is now garbage, the others he re-boxes and marks them with a check so anyone who uses them will know the protective layer has already been peeled.

He closes the van door and then opens it again. The light is dull, nearly out.

"Shit," he says.

In the house, the exterminator cleans what little mess there is out of the bathroom. He walks to the kitchen, where the couple sits at a modern table that seems out of place in a house full of old furniture.

"Coffee?" the woman says.

"I should get back to the office," the exterminator says. "Thanks, though."

She has the check book out. "What do we owe you?"

"No need to worry about that now," he says. "Billing handles all the money. It's fifty for the visit, plus the rate for whatever was killed. You do get a five percent discount, though."

"Why?" the man says.

"January," the exterminator says. "Rat is the pest of the month." Which is true. Every month, on the billboard outside the office, there is a five foot by ten foot poster of the pest of the month.

The exterminator once had a dream where he drove to work, saw himself on the billboard, and was gassed by fellow employees.

"That's nice." The woman pauses. "I guess."

The couple thanks the exterminator as he leaves. He gives a little wave and walks to the van. More snow has fallen, is falling, and he stands again for a moment in the quiet motion.

He gets in the van and turns the key. The engine hints at turning over and then abandons itself. The exterminator turns the key again. The engine turns a little less. By the third turn of the key, the sound is reduced to a click. The exterminator surprises himself by not being angered at this. He steps out of the van and stands again in the snow.

The exterminator will:

In a moment, go inside and ask for a jump.

Go to the office.

Dump the rat and glue strip off to be cremated.

Log his hours.

Go home.

Feed Fausto.

Drink coffee.

Take a shower.

Watch TV.

Wait for his phone to ring.

Want a drink.

Read.

Listen to the clock tick beside his bed.

Try to sleep.

Read.

Listen to his heartbeat.

End up back at work tomorrow, killing things to pay the rent, driving around in a giant rat.

He will do all of these things, he is sure. But for now, the exterminator stands motionless in the swirling whiteness, unsure of his next step, looking up toward the source of the storm.

Love and Hope and Sex and Dreams

My mother flies the Rolling Stones to New York and back three times a week in a private plane they've leased out of the Oxford Airport. They rehearse for their tour in Connecticut, but they need to be in the city often enough to rent their own plane.

She tells me this over the phone. I'm on my back porch in California, collecting disability and not doing much of anything and my mother is the Rolling Stones' private pilot.

"Charlie," she says. "The quiet one. The guitarist?"

"Drummer," I say.

"Drummer," she says. "He's very nice."

And as she talks, I wonder:

How did this happen? How did my mom get a cooler life than me?

My elbow, or what used to be my elbow, is killing me. I'm in a soft cast now after twelve weeks in hard plaster that ran from beneath the shoulder to the wrist. They fused the two major bones in the right arm so that it no longer moves.

Before the surgery, the doctor asked me what position I'd like my arm to be fixed in. There was a choice, you see.

I asked Lynn what she thought.

"It's your arm," she said.

I told her that since she had to look at it and be with it, that I felt it was her arm as well, in a way. Since it wouldn't be useful in any way we were accustomed to, in what position would it serve us best?

"It'd look better in a suit if it were straight," she said.

"I don't wear suits." I said.

"It'd be more practical for fucking if it were bent."

And so it's fused at something resembling a right angle. A no-brainer.

My lawyer calls and tells me the disability pay will keep up until I'm dead. The accident was their fault—the contractor doesn't argue this—and I can't paint again, at least not the way I did.

This is my life now. People call me. I'm on the back porch drinking—they hope and I assure them—something non-alcoholic. Haven't had a drink in one year and three hundred and fifty-five days. I count it off every morning. Still, it's a question everybody asks when they call.

I'm on the porch, I tell them.

I don't know what I'm going to do with the rest of my life, I tell them.

I'm healing, I tell them. Up until a few weeks ago, I'd knock on the plaster so they could hear it. This morning, when my mother called, I hit the soft cast and it let off a squishy thuck.

My arm is a dead fish. I bang it on things—doorjambs, tables, the edges of the house—and it thuck, thuck, thucks like Ringo Starr's tom toms in "A Day in the Life." Sounds dead and warm at the same time.

The sun is directly overhead. Hot. Leaves go back and forth with and against the wind. Some birds scatter shadows over the deck and I lie back and close my eyes. The shadows, I can still sort of feel them.

Lynn's home. I hear her in the kitchen thumping bags down on the counter. My eyes are still closed, but I know what's going on. I can see the cat hopping up onto the kitchen table, can see her rub the bags with her head. Lynn comes out on the deck—I hear the door stick—and I open my eyes. I blink a few times and get used to the light.

"How you feeling?" she says.

"Same," I say. "How was work?"

She lifts my legs off the chair I'm resting them on, sits down and puts my legs over her lap.

"I think my mother's having an affair," she says.

"No."

She lights a cigarette and smiles. "You know Jimmy Duggan? Friend of my dad's?"

"Don't think so," I say.

"Doesn't matter," she says. Lynn's got a bunch of bangles on her left arm, rings on every finger. When she's excited about something, she taps. She's tapping now on the deck table. Tap, tap, jangle, jangle. Festive. My wife is a mariachi band with a story to tell.

"I call her this morning—my mother—and I hear a voice in the background. A man's voice."

"What time?" I say.

"Nine-thirty, ten. Dad's at work by then. So I say, 'Who's there, Mom?' and she says, 'No one's here. Why do ask?' And I say that I heard a voice and she interrupts me and says, 'Lynn—no one is here.' So I'm like OK, OK, and we talk for a couple minutes, hang up, and I get back to work."

"That's it?" I say.

She has a sip of her beer. Taps, jangles. Shakes her head.

"No," she says. "About twenty minutes later, my phone rings I pick it up and my mother says, 'No one's here, Lynn.' And I tell her OK, fine, I believe her. No one's there. And she says, 'You don't believe me? Come over. No one's here.'"

"She invited you down?" I say.

"Like I can take an hour off work," she says. "So I tell her that I believe her, I don't need to come down and at this point she's on the verge of tears says, over and over, 'You don't believe me, you don't believe me.' So I say, 'Mom, I believe you. No one's there.' Eventually we hang up and I go back to work." She takes another sip of beer. "Five, maybe ten minutes later, the phone rings again."

"Your mother?"

She nods. "Mom. And she says—very quiet." My wife pauses, and mimes that she's got a phone to her ear. "'Lynn,' she says. 'Jimmy was here. Jimmy Duggan. But we were just having breakfast,' and she hangs up."

"Really?"

"Really. Mom's a shitty liar. I think an affair would be good for her, though." She shudders as if a cold breeze had hit the porch. "But Jimmy Duggan. Yeash." She knocks her knuckles on my shin. "How was your day?"

"My mother's flying the Rolling Stones from Connecticut to New York and back three days a week," I tell her.

She looks at me.

"Really," I say.

The night we were married, my wife and I stayed at a posh hotel in Salt Lake City. The room was on the eleventh floor, as high as I've ever slept in my life. Late, in bed, I asked her why she had two pillows and I only had one.

"Because they only gave us three," she said.

I envy my wife. She's smart, smarter than me, and I'm one of the smartest people you'll ever meet, and she seems—most of the time—to know what she wants.

Me? No idea. I've always complained I didn't have time to do things. Now I've got nothing but time. I sit on my porch and take phone calls.

My neighbor's gardener, who's deaf, has taken to cleaning my neighbor's yard by tossing branches and leaves onto my back deck. I sit and watch, my eyes focused on the top of the fence; branches break into my line of vision and fall on the deck by the grill.

When I was still in the hard cast, I'd get up and toss them back over. Me and the deaf gardener went like that for hours one day——back and forth—tossing the same branches. A couple days later, I get a letter from my neighbor telling me to stop harassing his gardener. At the bottom of the note, he wrote—"The man is old and deaf for God's sake."

I've let it go for now. My plan—long range, to be sure, but effective—is to never again cut the spider-infested Twisted Juniper that hangs from my deck to his backyard. He has a problem with bugs, and I'm no longer in a hurry.

Branches fall, gently crash on my side.

"You've got to hear this," Lynn says from the open door out to the deck.

"What?"

"Hurry. The TV's picking up something fun."

When Lynn works at home, she keeps this TV on in her office. An old black and white that for years has picked up CB conversations. The last six months, since they put in the transmitter outside town by the highway, it picks up cellular phone calls.

The picture's been shot for years—no vertical hold, no horizontal, and almost total darkness on the screen. Wavy dark figures flip by. A slot machine and a funhouse mirror in one. How she works with it on is beyond me. The noise of the TV gets interrupted by phone calls and CB's the way they announce track numbers at the train station. Breaks in, all sudden and loud.

"And what are you doing to me?" A man's voice says.

"You're tied to the ceiling," a woman's voice says. "I've slipped a two-by-four under your heels, and when your heels barely touch the wood I kick it out so you're on your toes, hands above your head."

Lynn looks at me, raises her eyebrows and grins. She's Groucho Marx. Me? I'm Harpo, mute, smiling. She taps her rings. She whispers to me: "His name's Eric. She's Mistress Carly."

"Yes," the man named Eric says. "Then?"

"Then I whip you. Have you ever been whipped?"

"No," Eric says. He sounds hurt, disappointed.

"It stings," Mistress Carly says.

"I like her," Lynn says. "She sounds hot."

"And after I'm done whipping you, I leave you tied where you are and have one of my slaves wipe rubbing alcohol on your wounds," Mistress Carly says.

"You have slaves?" Eric says. "You're for real?"

"I'm real," Mistress Carly says. There's a pause. She says: "Are you married?"

"Yes," Eric says.

"You should tell your wife," Mistress Carly says. "She might surprise you."

"I don't know," Eric says.

Mistress Carly starts to say something, but the voices are cut off by some trucker out on the highway. A burst of noise, followed by a mixture of voice and static. The regular voices from the TV show come back.

Back on the deck, the sun begins to go down over the ocean. The smog makes for beautiful sunsets. People talk about how wonderful nature is, but smog and chemical waste bring more color out of an evening sky. True. LA County and Gary, Indiana have the best sunsets in the world. I've been just about everywhere and I know.

When I said that I was one of the smartest people you'll ever meet, I wasn't lying. I wasn't, and this is important, bragging either. Way I see it, being the smartest person in a room doesn't mean a whole hell of a lot.

Most humans are too dumb to live. We're ill-equipped. I know a few languages, can talk with the best of them. I could give an articulate Marxist reading of a tube of Aqua-Fresh. When I talk, what do I do? I juggle air, I spin plates of vapor. I can keep more meaningless things in my head than most. Facts are facts. None of them are answers to anything.

September 15, 1830: a person is killed by a moving train for the first time.

At the top of the Empire State Building on a clear autumn day, you will be hit by barley that has flown 1,200 miles from Nebraska.

The animal with the highest blood pressure on earth is the giraffe.

These are facts.
Be a genius; see what it gets you.

My cousin calls. He asks what's up and I tell him that my finger-nails are growing for the first time in my life. I hang up. The finger-nail thing is true; I bite them until they're bloody little torn things. I can no longer reach my right hand to my mouth. The nails grow and grow. They're snake skins at the end of my hand. They curl; translucent and colorful at the same time.

My cousin is a dolt. He called because he wanted something and, this time, I was smart enough to cut it off before he got to his point.

You know my cousin. He's got everything figured out. He says shit like: "The fact-of-the-matter-," and "What you've got to under-stand is—". He defends the government. He's an arrogant traffic cop; he swaggers through life.

In bed, Lynn says: "I picture her as a sort of Emma Peel."
   "Who?"
   "Emma Peel, from 'The Avengers'."
   "I know who Emma Peel is," I say. "Who are you talking about?"
   "Mistress Carly," she says.
   "Why Emma Peel?" I say.
   She shrugs. "She was a hot, take-charge kind of gal. I had a thing for Emma Peel when I was young."
   "Who didn't?"
   "Plus those great outfits. Bet that's what she looks like."
   "Could be," I say.

Three in the morning. Lynn's asleep. I've always had trouble at night, even when I was working. It's gotten worse since the accident. I flip through the channels; see what's on. Nothing much, a bunch of infomercials—most of them diet stuff. You know the kind; take our pill and lose weight; use our machine and lose weight.

I read somewhere that Americans spend 32 billion dollars a year on the diet industry. So what, right? I'm full of facts; I know things.

Last week, when I couldn't sleep in our bed, I came out to the couch. I do that sometimes. Once, twice a month I need to sleep on the couch; once a year I sleep in the car. It's something I need to do.

I'm a bastard to live with. The accident's no excuse. I've been like this since I can remember.

One time, at a party, Lynn said: "We like eggplant." And I went ballistic on her. Told her that I liked eggplant and she liked eggplant, but we—this single-celled creature of oneness that couples become—didn't like anything. I lectured her like a child. Made an ass out of myself. This was in front of friends. She didn't speak with me for three days.

This is years ago, the eggplant fight. I think about it when I can't sleep. This is regret. This is me, what I do. I hate the me that comes out when we fight. Those times, she deserves better and I deserve worse.

Some professor is talking about space with Charlie Rose. "A black hole is created," he says, "when gravity becomes more powerful than the escaping energy." He, too, is full of facts.

"What would it look like?" Charlie Rose says. "To be inside?"

"Inside?" the professor says. "Gravity would be so powerful as to make time slow down. If you could see out, people would age a lifetime in a nanosecond." He takes a drink of water. "This is a theory, though. There is no light in the hole. There would be nothing to see." He pauses. "Or, rather, we couldn't see anything."

"What's the difference?" Charlie Rose says.

"In reality, very little. But it's a key theoretical distinction," the professor says.

I try the TV in Lynn's office. Nothing too interesting there, either. No fun phone calls. The cop CB channel breaks in with a liquor store owner killed in Long Beach; some trucker with an illegal load wants to make it to Salt Lake City by noon and asks for suggested back roads where he won't get weighed. Someone tells him to get off the fifteen at Big Rock Candy Mountain and head north.

Out on the deck, I listen to Hank William's *The Great Thirty-Eight* and read the *Sporting News NBA Guide*, which has the statistics of every National Basketball Association player from 1946 to the present. Team-by-team stats for everyone who ever played in the league.

Lynn asked me once how I could read numbers.

"What's in numbers that could possibly interest you?" was how she put it.

And I explained that they weren't numbers. In the 1975-76 season, Walt Frazier—great point guard of the New York Knicks—played in only 59 of a possible 82 regular season games. The 23 games he missed isn't a number, not to me anyway.

His mother died that year in Atlanta, for one thing. He also got a bad hip-pointer—the first serious injury of his career—and lost his quickness moving laterally. Frazier was never the same player. In three years, he was out of the league.

There's a story there—for every 23 games missed, a lifetime could pass. If there is such a thing as a true story, numbers may tell a truer one than the truth itself.

The numbers say Hank Williams was twenty-nine years old when he died in his limo.

The number the coroner came up with, upon opening him up and inspecting what was left, was between forty-five and fifty. That's what it looked like—opened on that table—an old, dead man.

Hank croons "I'm So Lonesome I Could Cry." Planes fly overhead. The low ones are coming into LA; the high ones are headed out. People up there. Lives. I read numbers, try to make sense out of things to pass the time. Hank moans on.

When I drank, I told a hell of a lot of stories. Lies, for the most part. Get enough gin in me, and I'd give you my song and dance, tell you about my years putting out oil fires, my high-security rating with the CIA, ask you if you'd ever heard the sound of a man's neck snapping.

Did you know, I'd ask, that the only way to tell a real sapphire from a fake sapphire is to heat them both to a thousand degrees and hit them both with a steel rod? The real one disintegrates.

That one, as far as I know, is true. A good friend of mine, Francois—witness at our wedding—told me about it. He's full of facts, too, but his facts comfort me more than most.

Mostly, though, I lied. Told my stories, drank, and moved every two years.

The thing about the sound of a man's neck snapping—I do know that sound, though it wasn't me who did the snapping.

About ten years ago, I was on a road crew. A government job for big money. We were contracted to paint new yellow and white lines through Nebraska and Wyoming. Federal work on Route. 80. We also had to put a fresh coat of magnetic paint on all the major bridges. The job was almost a full year, interrupted by the winter.

One day, west of the North Platte River, we're painting and a coffee-colored van with Indiana plates comes barrel-assing into the construction lane and hits Sal Roma, one of the older guys on the crew. The van sends him up in the air and he falls in a clump; a mixed pool of blood, piss and shit under and around him. The van goes off the road and sits—half sideways—in a ditch of weeds.

Some of the crew head to Sal, but me and this guy Hollis go over to the van. The driver's middle-aged, maybe forty-five. He's still conscious, his head bleeds from a gash on the temple.

"He'll live," I say.

And Hollis reaches into the driver's side and twists the guy's head like he's a big bottle of beer. The neck makes a few strained noises and lets go like a thick branch snapping under too much weight. The driver's head slumps to his chest. He's a dead bird, eyes unfocused, head at some crazy angle.

Hollis looks at me and I nod.

We walk back up to the shoulder where Sal Roma landed. Paramedics are on their way.

"How the driver?" the crew chief says.

I shrug, look away. Hollis says: "Doesn't look so good."

Sal Roma's down on the tarmac and I notice for the first time the van cut through fresh paint and there are white tire tracks leading into the ditch.

Sal's on his back, his face white. The blood's already drained down out of him and settled in his body close to the road. His face and the top of his arms are the moon at night; the part of him close to the road is purple-black. Airbrushed and shiny; he's a two-tone Custom Harley.

Hollis? I worked with him for another two, three months and he never spoke to me. I never knew much about him, only that he killed that driver and he walked through life with two misspelled tattoos. "I Eat Pusy." And "Unbirdled."

I was in a drunk tank once with a guy who had "I can," tattooed over one eyelid in English and "see you," over the other in Spanish.

Lynn takes the afternoon off and drives me to the doctor.

"Eric told his wife," she says. She lights a cigarette, taps and jangles against the steering wheel. "Just heard him and Mistress Carly on the TV."

"And?"

"She left him," Lynn says.

"Poor guy."

She nods and taps, looks straight ahead. "Twelve months of hell," she says.

And I nod and repeat: "Twelve months of hell." Our refrain for breakups.

The doctor takes the soft cast off and tries to break some of the adhesions. The arm is blue, purple, yellow, a rainbow bruise. I look at this arm; I think of death.

That little ball-shaped bone on your wrist? Biggest thing on the arm, now that all the muscle's gone. A golf ball under the skin. The adhesions pop and burn; little carpenter's nails do somersaults in the arm.

"Why are we doing this?" I say. There will be no range of motion; that much has been assured.

"So you can feel your fingers," the doctor says. She's trying to do her job. She pops two more.

I say OK, but I'm still unclear on how this will aid me in life—knowing that it hurts when I bump this lifeless thing against the door jamb versus not knowing that it hurts.

"Are you going to cut these nails?" she says. She points to my snakeskins.

I lift my shoulders, a pantomime of apathy.

"Yes," Lynn says. "He is."

On the way home, Lynn says: "When are you going to do something?"

I have no answer.

We get home and there's a message from my mother. Keith Richards gave her a hundred dollar tip this morning as he got off the plane. There's an FAA law, she explains, that says planes that seat fewer than twelve people cannot have alcohol on them. She waived this rule and allowed Keith Richards to have his bottle of Rebel Yell with him for the trip. He gave her the hundred. Keith Richards said: "Thanks, Luv," to my mom and got off the plane.

He's a gentleman, my mother tells our machine.

Everything we buy, we decide right off who gets it in the divorce. Lynn's idea. Once a month, we have a meeting where we make a case for the marriage. A list of pros and cons. So far, we've stuck it out. I love my wife.

My biggest fear?

An image. We're both old, much older than now, and we'll have nothing, absolutely nothing, to say to one another. And I'll see her eyes drift off, thinking about how her life could have been better. I fear a longing that doesn't include me.

Out on the deck, a chain of ants moves beneath me. It's like a highway; some go one way, some the other. Little black dots of traffic. I'm the helicopter. I spit in their path and miss. A second shot lands—splat—in their little highway. A few of them stumble around. Most keep moving. Relentless creatures.

Tomorrow, I will get two phone calls.

I'll be out on the deck, playing crippled god to a highway of ants. The first call will be from my doctor and she'll tell me that I missed my nine o'clock.

"Yes," I'll say. "I did."

"You'll lose that hand," she'll say. "All motion. All feeling."

And I'll apologize and reschedule for another appointment that I may or may not miss.

The second call will be from Lynn, though she won't say who she is. I'll recognize the voice.

"I think I'm leaving my husband," the voice will say.

"Really?" I will say. I'm watching my ants running their patterns. "Why?"

"It's not so much a question of why," she'll say, "as it's a question of why not."

And we're playing a game, but we're not. "Does he know?" I say.

And this stranger on the phone will tell me about her husband, about a man who listens to Hank Williams and reads numbers as if they were all sad stories. This man who watches planes go overhead and says how depressing they are.

And I nod. I watch branches fly from my neighbor's yard onto my deck; I hear the grunts of a deaf gardener.

"Are you still there?" she says.

"I'm still here," I say.

"Well? What do you think? Should I leave him?" she says.

I met Lynn when I was still drinking. I was on a crew doing some painting outside LA County. It was mostly road work. She wore torn blue jeans, silver-tipped cowboy boots, and a black silk top. We talked a lot—she talked, I bullshitted—we told stories.

She was, at that time, the third in a ménage a trios with a married couple in Santa Monica.

She told me the couple she was with stopped going on vacations together because one was a Calvinist sightseer and the other was a strict Lacanian and I knew I was in love.

When I drank, I was that fiddle you hear in country music. Sloppy, melancholy, pathetic. Not without charm in small doses.

"Are you there?" the voice will say again.

I finger my dead fish of an arm and try to decide whether or not to make a case for this husband of hers.

Swiss Engineering

I enter my brother Skip's Volvo into the Crawford Raceway's Saturday Night Amateur Demolition Derby. I'm dizzy from the heat and the fact that I've had, maybe, five hours sleep in the last five days.

"What is that?" Loomis Crawford, son of Darrell 'Big Daddy' Crawford, says from his booth.

"For the derby," I say.

"I know what it's *for*," he says and drums his pen on his clipboard. He's got rhythm, Gene Krupa with a sunburn registering wrecked cars. "I need to know where it goes. It needs a slot."

"A slot?"

"Where are Volvo's from?"

"It's Swiss," I say.

Loomis lights a cigarette. He looks at the car. "They make cars?"

"I think it's Swiss. Scandinavian, maybe. It's European, pretty sure of that much."

Loomis looks at the clipboard, taps, shakes his head. "For our purposes, it's an 'Other'. Got no Volvo slot."

"No Volvo slot," I repeat, nodding.

"You haven't done this before, have you?"

"No, sir. Seen it. Haven't done it."

"We got some paperwork for you to sign." He hands me the clipboard. "First one is the entry fee. I'll need fifty bucks with that, check's OK with a local address and phone. Second one there is the transfer of ownership. If you've got the pinks, that makes life easier all the way around. The last one says you can't sue us if you get seriously fucked up out there."

"Got it. But Volvo's are the safest cars there are." I sign the papers and give him fifty in cash. The car that saves lives—that's how Volvo marketed these in the '70s. A cabin that could withstand the worst of collisions, brakes that stop on a dime, a car that saves lives. "I have a distinct advantage," I say, thinking of those old ads.

"Right."

"You don't think it's weird, me putting a car this nice in the derby?" I say.

Loomis looks at the car, then at me. "Not that nice a car. I figure you got your reasons."

"You ever had anyone get hurt too bad?"

"Bad enough," Loomis says. "We give you a helmet. Anything else, elbow pads, flack jacket, you got to rent that."

My first day in Destin, in my disguise, I looked like a beat up gold prospector, like Walter Huston in *The Treasure of Sierra Madre*. I sat in a chair and snapped four pictures of myself with a Polaroid One-Step—two facing dead on, one in left profile, one in right. Sat in the turbocharged air-conditioning and watched these strange images—me but not me—swell up on 3x5 paper. I had the Dream Syndicate's great album *The Days of Wine and Roses* on constant repeat, blaring loud enough for the neighbors to complain.

I scanned the two best pictures into my lap top, played cut and paste for a while until I came up with the ad. Across the top, it reads *HAVE YOU SEEN THIS MAN?* and then the photos. Beneath the photos reads:

"Last seen August 9th, in the Piggly Wiggly Parking Lot. He may be lost and disoriented. Do not approach him. Please call the Sea Breeze Motel, room #6 with any information. My brother is very sick and confused. Reward."

Destin, Florida is a little clam-strip of land stuck on the panhandle—known locally as the 'Redneck Riviera'. It holds little to brag about, except for Saturday nights at 'Big Daddy' Crawford's racetrack. Five years ago, when I was living in Sarasota, I had a painting job twenty miles south of here at a condo development. Three weeks in heat so bad our plastic buckets melted and we had to transfer the paint to metal buckets that blistered your hands. Three Saturdays running, my crew and I headed up here to Destin and watched the races.

The first nine are legit, country crackers come out of the woodwork with their cars—some from Gulf towns, some from southern horse towns like Ocala. The first three races are midgets, the next six are homemade stocks. The last race of the night is the derby. For fifty bucks, anyone with a car they don't mind destroying and who signs the waver can enter. The last car running splits the collected entry fees with Big Daddy. On a slow night, there are about ten cars. A good summer night, like tonight, could draw twenty.

I got to town a week ago and placed the missing person ad on every box and wall I could find in Destin. Every day, I've gone out in the disguise that matches the ads. In the afternoon, I come back to the Sea Breeze and wait for the phone calls.

The third day, I ventured out in the disguise and went to the Piggly Wiggly, did some shopping. Went to the post office. I do all of this riding a bike in hopes that I'd be easier to spot and find out that there are an awful lot of men—looking anywhere from 30 to 50 in age—that pedal around the town. Beaten men. Thin, scraggly Harry Dean Stanton clones ride with their shirts off, tied around their waists. Sad creatures. At the post office, I ask the clerk why so many men are on bikes.

"DUI rate," she says and doesn't look up. "Highest in the state. You're seeing drunks."

"I'm seeing drunks?" I say, understanding what she said, but not quite the way she said it.

"The bikes," she says. "Drunks."

"The glass?" I say to Loomis Crawford.

"Windows. Windshield. They got to go."

"Really?"

"We'll do it for you," he says. "Ten bucks."

"No," I say. "I can do it." I look at the cream-colored Volvo and its tinted glass. All leather interior, AC, disc stereo—Skip must've dumped thirty grand on this thing.

"I'll rent you a bat for five," Loomis says.

"I'll use the wheel wrench," I say.

"Suit yourself," he says. "Take a tip, though. Work inside out."

"Why?"

"One, glass is made to take external pressure—it's a lot easier to pop from the interior. Two, you don't want to be grinding your back and balls in cut glass during the derby."

That third day, after the post office, I get my first call. It sounds like an old woman with a June Cleaver voice.

"I think I've seen your brother," she says.

"Come again?"

"The man on the poster," she says. "Your brother. I've seen him, I'm pretty sure."

"My brother's dead," I tell her. "He had a tumor in his head the size of a grapefruit," I lie. "What kind of sick fuck are you?"

She begins to say something and I hang up on her. I picture her in her kitchen, the phone still in her hand. June Cleaver confused. June Cleaver just-trying-to-help. June Cleaver losing out on her reward money. And I hate her. I hate all of them.

The calls kept coming, all the way up until today. *My brother's dead*, I told them all. *Is this some kind of sick joke*? I said. *You're evil,* I said. The good people of Destin, Florida don't know what hit them.

The tumor in my brother's head—which bulged to walnut-sized, not grapefruit-sized, just before his surgery and death—gave him these things called *fugues*. Death, dying and hospitals give you new words. Before my brother grew a walnut in his head, the only fugues

I'd ever heard of were the musical ones, as in Mozart's *Toccata en* . . . Before this, too, I always had trouble remembering which was bad, benign or malignant. When he was diagnosed, I asked Skip which was which. They both sounded bad enough and what, after all, is a good tumor?

He said, "One grows from the roof of the cave, one grows from the floor." I thought back to trips with our folks to Luray Caverns and the Lost Sea and the transparent fish with the neon feelers jutting out of their little heads. "It's bad," he said. "You're talking to a dead man, Bro. Maybe you were right," he said and hung up.

What I was right—or maybe right—about was being the fuckup he always accused me of being. This was Skip feeling—justifiably—sorry for himself. Thinking, if he was going to die at forty-two anyway, he should've been more like Ben. Should have screwed around, gotten drunk, flunked some classes. Thinking maybe he shouldn't have been so good, for so many years.

These fugues, Skip had three of them before he died. They're, from what I gathered, like waking blackouts. Not like Alzheimer's—the person functions—you can work, drive, talk; go through your life, basically. And then *snap* you come to and you don't remember a thing.

The worst, Skip told me, was when he woke up in an abandoned strip-mall parking lot at three in the morning. It had rained and he was wet; pools of neon danced in puddles. He'd lost two days.

"Two days," he said to me on the phone. "Lost."

I told him that I'd read in Harper's Index that there were only two cases of amnesia in the US last year, but that there were four hundred and seventy-two on daytime TV.

"Not quite the same," he said.

And I wanted to say I *know* it's not, but I'm trying here.

This all came to me after the funeral and the reading of the will where I got Skip's Volvo. My sister-in-law, Judy, and the kids got the house and the other car and everything they need. I got the Volvo—which I don't need or want—and I know right away that it's not a car, it's a message from Skip. *Be responsible*, it says. *Take care of something for once.* My brother had a way of giving unfriendly gifts—the kind of guy who gives his wife an exercise cycle for her birthday. Skip and I could never really talk to each other. I loved him—he was my brother—and if I didn't dislike him, I never liked him much, either.

I thought *what am I going to do with this car*? and it all came to me. Not like a plan, not step-by-step, but all at once like a safe falling on my head. I'm at the lawyers and cha-ching, all hell breaks loose in my head and I get these cartoon one-arm-bandit eyes that keep coming up wrecked Volvos. Something inside me said go to Destin, place missing person ads and enter the car in the Derby. By the time I thought about it, really thought about it, I'd already driven up from Miami.

I'm in the passenger seat, both boots kicking at the driver side window and I get this rush that I haven't let myself feel before this. I kick out the window, scoot over to the driver side and kick out the other one. I'm running on some hollow momentum and something inside me is punching itself out. There are words for this: sorrow, regret, pain. There are no words for this. You know this feeling; every table in the world just had its legs knocked out from under it and things keep falling. From the backseat, I kick twice at the rear window and it resists and fights against me until it comes off in one piece, and flops down on the trunk.

Loss precedes words is the way I've come to understand things. The first time I'd ever heard of an anterior cruciate ligament was when a doctor told me mine was torn—popped so bad that one side of it had nothing to do with the other side. I'm number two scorer—all-time—in Florida college basketball history behind Rick Barry. Look it up—Ben Thompson behind Barry, ahead of everybody else. I didn't know I had an anterior cruciate until I lost it, didn't know I had a future until I didn't. Skip was a dead man before the doctors said *tumor,* and before they said *malignant,* and was walking like a zombie through his days before he'd ever heard of a *fugue.* The damage was done; the naming came later.

And I don't know who I am right now with this missing persons/demolition derby stunt. But I'm not Ben Thompson who rained down jump shots at Miami, not Ben Thompson ex-drunk, not Ben Thompson commercial & residential painter. Not Ben, Skip's brother. There is a fracture and I'll come up with names for this. All that will come because that's the way it has worked in the past.

It's past midnight when the derby gets going. Hot, still over ninety, and the kind of muggy where you draw in breath, you feel moisture. There's me and fifteen other cars, all big American models from the '60s and '70s. They're beat-up. I look out, I see an ocean of mud, exhaust, sunburns and gray primer. Big Daddy calls the race. The crowd's restless and itching for the demolition. There were fewer accidents than usual in the preliminary races and the blood lust of Destin is high. You can feel it. They want to see pain.

I look at this mass of sweating losers and I get the same feeling I had on the phone when June Cleaver called. Why not them? These ugly, lousy people. Who would miss them? Why Skip with his kids and his wife and people who care whether he lived or died? I'm revving the Volvo in neutral, wearing a green metallic helmet they gave me, no pads or jacket

The gun is fired to start the derby and I slip the Volvo into first, circling the track. The car's rear end thuds, the sound of crushed and bent steel thunders all over the dirt. One after the other, you can hear the jolts. I'm feeling them too. It's like bumpercars on a big scale. I'm backed into three times by this clown in an early '70s Duster before I can react.

Something changes and this is a game. A movie. I'm poor-boy Elvis, a struggling singer/demolition derby driver and Shelly Fabres/ Natalie Wood/Ann Margaret is waiting for me in my moment of triumph. A soundtrack clicks into my head and I'm laughing and crying and I'm in first gear, violating rule number one which is always, always back into your opponent to save your engine. I smash the guy in the Duster in the driver side door and he bolts one way and then the other like JFK in the Zapruder film. Snap, snap, and he's gone down on the front seat.

I take five more cars out solo—other damage is going on around me and cars are dropping. The track is a mix of mud and oil and gas and it smells like the world's on fire. All of this is covered in a burning smell. They stop the race when a white flag comes out of the driver's side door, indicating the car's dead. The driver gets out, the car stays on the dirt and the race goes on. I whiz around the twisted wreckage hitting anything I see—car with drivers, cars without drivers—until it's down to me and two other cars.

I slide the Volvo into reverse and wait for these last two to make a move. They, separately, independently, do the same. You can hear the crowd. I'm covered in sweat, my eyes sting and I have to blink every couple of seconds to clear the salt and smoke from them. A million bugs are on me. My skin's thick and hard and heavy from the bites, like ten tetanus shot on each arm. Big Daddy calls the three remaining cars into the center.

"Take a lap, each of you," he says. Then in one of those Wrestle-mania voices, he says, "And let's GET IT ON." The crowd, maybe two hundred tired drunks, cheers.

I take my lap. I'm ready to kill these last two bastards. Their cars aren't enough. All-American poor-boy Elvis—it's become clear to me—has come to Destin, Florida to put a hurting on someone.

What I'm hoping is that this is going to be like one of Skip's fugues. That I'll wake up in some parking lot or hotel room or restaurant and will remember none of what's happening here. That something ugly has attached itself to my head, is growing inside me, is fucking me up. I want this. I want lost days.

The Volvo's speedometer's broken, but it feels like I'm doing twenty when a primer-gray Vista Cruiser station wagon, the kind you only see these days at college graduations, whacks into my front end. Something in my neck pops, I hear it and feel it, and there's blood coming from my forehead. Blood's in my right eye and I blink and blink and blink and all I get is a wet film the color of blush wine. Smoke and fluid are spewing up out of the front end. The car won't budge. The two cars gang up on what's left of me and I'm bouncing like a ping-pong ball between their rear bumpers.

I don't put the white flag out. Not yet, anyway. The car jolts back and forth and I sit back and try to clear my eyes with the back of my sweat-covered hand. There's smoke everywhere—different color smoke—gray exhaust, the black shit coughing from under the hood. Dirt, burnt oil and smoke rise and settle on me and everything else. My foot won't move and I think my ankle might be broken. The cars keep hitting me, and I sit still, seeing just how safe this Volvo is. Seeing what these Swiss or Scandinavian—or whatever the fuck Europeans they are—have come up with.

Burn Ward

It's after visiting hours and neither of us can sleep. Marty and I stay up skimming through an old *Cosmopolitan* one of the volunteers left. He can't move, so I do the reading.

He's in this contraption called a Striker Frame that rotates and keeps pressure off all parts of the body. He looks like a mummy stuck in the middle of an enormous gyroscope. It leaves him suspended, looking down.

"Is there a quiz?"

"Yeah," I say, trying to find something else to read.

"Let's do it," he says. "I'm in a quiz mood."

I take a breath. "OK. It's called 'What Is Your Body Language Telling Him?'"

He laughs, but I still feel funny. "So, you want me to read this?"

"Sure? How could I take offense? No body language here. Not much anyway." He laughs, quieter this time. "I just shrugged. You missed it."

Marty works, or worked, in an auto body shop. He's here because of a leak in an oxygen tank. Lit his torch and the whole room went up. It took the nurses two days to soak what was left of his shirt from what was left of his skin.

I'm here because I rolled my bike on the Route 25 connector. Blew a tire and went face down on the tarmac. Lost my nose. They rebuilt it using cartilage from my knee and skin from my shoulder.

That was after the knee surgery. Now I'm on the burn ward in a hip-to-ankle cast and a heavy gauze wrap around most of my head.

I'm not a burn victim, but this is where they send anyone who needs, or got, a skin graft. I lucked out, really. Lost a lot of skin, but not so much that they couldn't replace it from other parts of my body. Marty has to wait for them to get skin compatible to his own. They take sample tissue from the recently dead, usually from the ER The process is called harvesting.

"Question five. You're at a bar. The woman is on your left, her right leg crossed over her left. She's turned slightly toward you."

"On the edge of her stool, as it were?"

"Stop interrupting," I say. "She's resting her head on the back of both hands. Now, what does her body language suggest to you?"

"I don't know," Marty says. "She sounds a little fru-fru to me. That back of the hands bit." He breathes and the Striker Frame rocks a little. "What's she wearing?"

"Doesn't say."

"Miniskirt and garter belt?"

"If you want."

"This woman, does she have a name?"

"Not in the quiz."

"Let's make her Faye Dunaway," he says.

"You going to answer the question?"

"Just want to get all the details worked out. So Faye is on my left, turned slightly toward me, her right leg crossed over her left—let's scratch that hands bit."

"Fine. What does her body language tell you?"

"I'd say, and I don't mean to brag, but I'd say it means Faye Dunaway wants me."

"Cosmo agrees."

"Lucky me," he says.

Late nights, there's not much to do except talk, read, or watch TV I can only read for about a half-hour at a time before my eyes go crazy. Same with the television. If my eyes stay in one place too long, I get these vicious migraines. It's a side effect from the accident. Some sort of pressure on the brain that's supposed to go away in time.

I click through the channels and stop on an old Kojak episode. Marty watches the mirror rested on an angle against the wall he faces.

"Stay," he says. "I like cop shows."

"I know a woman who went down on Telly Savalas for a gram of cocaine in Atlantic City," I say.

"Get out of town."

"No. Really."

"Don't believe it," he says.

"I dated her for a while. Jane Becker. She was pretty wild. I believed her. She wasn't the type to lie."

"Yeach. Change the station."

"Mind if I turn it off?" I say.

"In a minute. I want to see something else. It's a nasty image to go to sleep on."

"Who loves ya baby?"

"I'll never be able to watch Kojak again," he says.

Some sitcom's on.

"You know that most canned laughter is dead people?" Marty says.

"What?"

"The laugh track," he says. "Most laugh tracks they use on TV are tapes of the live audiences from the early fifties. Earnie Kovacs, Ed Sullivan, *The Honeymooners*. Shows like that."

"You sure?" I say. "Why would they use old tapes?"

"After television started taping episodes, the best way to simulate a live audience was to use the old tapes. Anyway, most of the people you hear laughing on TV are dead now."

"How do you know that?"

"Communications major."

"How'd you end up working on cars?" I say.

"Liberal arts education," he says. "Doesn't prepare you for much except for unique opportunities in the food service industry. I mean, what was your major?"

"English," I say.

"And what do you do?"

"Since I got out? Waited tables and painted houses. Same shit I did during the summers to pay for school."

The night nurse comes in and tells us it's time to go to sleep. Why it's up to her when we sleep, I haven't figured out yet. Well, it is up to her when Marty sleeps since she gives him a shot, some tranquilizer into the IV line.

The drugs used to give him strange dreams that we'd talk about to pass the time. The last couple nights, though, he's dreamed he was in the Striker Frame. Not much sense talking about that.

He's tried to sleep without the shot, but the pain from the burns keeps him up. I get no shot, and take this as a good sign. There's really no need. I'm not in much pain and, if the graft holds right, I won't be here much longer.

I flick through the channels, trying to think about what Marty said about the dead people laughing. It's interesting, that's all I can come up with. Interesting. No emotion, no sense. Since the accident, my powers of concentration are shot. It's like I have no control over them. Things I want to think about are kind of slippery.

Other things, memories, dreams, images, just spill in and out of my head. They hang around for a while and drift away.

Who was it that said most men lead lives of quiet desperation? If only it were true. There's some show on now with some movie star going on and on about his problems with pills and alcohol. Of course it wasn't his fault; he came from a dysfunctional family. The host is nodding, full of understanding.

"If I can help just one person out there . . . "

Right. And by the way my book, which is even more enlightening than this abridged tale of woe you've sat through, is only twenty bucks.

I buzz the nurse. She turns on the overhead light as she enters the room.

"Sorry to bother you," I say. "But could I get some more tissues?"

"You were lying down again, weren't you?" I nod. She walks out and comes back with a new box.

I'm not supposed to lie flat since they redid the nose three weeks ago. Both nostrils are plugged. At first, blood spilled to my throat, but now it's more like a normal runny nose.

I get to see it for the first time tomorrow. Later today, really. Marty and I have the same plastic surgeon, a guy not much older than either of us named Doctor Perkins. His age makes me nervous. I mean, I've never seen any of his work and it is my nose we're talking about. Marty calls him Skippy. Not when he's around, though. Better to not offend the man who's putting you back together.

I try to think of what I might look like when the wraps come off, but I can't focus on it. It's good, really, that I can stay put on one thought because there's plenty in here that I doubt I'd want to think about for too long.

On family trips when I was a kid, I used to sit in the rear of the station wagon. Places, objects, people would blur by and every once in a while my eyes would stop on something and I'd follow it until it disappeared. There, I would say to myself, focusing on the receding present, you were there.

That's sort of how my brain feels now—whizzing forward, looking backward and unable to stop on anything long enough to make sense of it.

"You still watching TV?" Marty says, startling me a little. I straighten up quickly and my knee twitches in pain. "Careful, it'll rot your brain."

"Too late for that," I say.

"You still getting headaches?"

"Yeah," I say. "If anything, they're worse. Getting a little worried about it." Which is true. At first I was far more worried about how I'd look after this, but now I'm beginning to wonder if I'll start thinking normal again. And if the pain'll go away. The more I try to concentrate, the more my head feels like I just ate ice cream too fast.

"Well," Marty says laughing quietly. "Try not to think about it too much."

"Fuck you."

"You still awake?" I say.

"Yup."

"How you feeling?"

"Like I should be in a bucket labeled 'Extra Crispy'. How about you?"

"OK. Little worried about tomorrow. Seeing the new nose." He doesn't say anything. "Sorry," I say.

"Why?"

"I just feel a little stupid complaining around you."

"Why? Because no matter how you come out of this, I'll be worse off than you?" He pauses and I look at the gauze wrap over his left hand. I saw what's left of the fingers once when they changed the dressing. The skin's all purple and the fingernails are deformed and bulging so they look like halved macadamia nuts.

"Right?" he says.

"That's part of it," I say. Which is true, it's only part of it. The other part is that I'll be getting out of here and it looks more and more like Marty may not. Which isn't my fault, but, still, I'm sorry about it.

"Well that's dumb," he says. "So there's people worse off than you. Big deal. There's people worse off than me. So you suffer, I suffer. So what? Throw a dart at the phone book and you'll hit someone who suffers." He laughs. Sort of a condescending laugh, but not mean-spirited.

"What?" I say.

"It's funny, that's all. Most people act as if they're the only person in the world who's ever suffered. Like it makes them special, unique. You? You act like you're not worthy of it. Like those liberals who as long as there's a child starving somewhere or a well-baby or whatever feel guilty about complaining that the phone bill's too high."

"I can't help it," I say. "I'm a guilt-ridden person."

"Well, you shouldn't be. It's stupid," he says. "Waste of energy." He pauses. "So," he says. "Complain."

"What?"

"Complain. Moan. Bitch, whine," he says. "It'll be good for you. Therapy."

"You're serious."

"Go ahead. What are you scared of? What are you worried about? What hurts?"

"My head hurts," I say.

"Good start. What else?"

"The knee. Yesterday, I moved my toes a little and it felt like someone ran a chainsaw all the way up the leg. The nose, or whatever it is under this wrap, hurts." I touch the bandage. I've been able to do that for about a week now. The whole thing's numb, feels like I'm touching someone, or something else. Which, in a way, I am.

"Go on," Marty says.

"That's about it," I say.

"You're lying."

"No. That's about it," I say. "Except for my head. Worried about that."

"The headaches?" he says.

"You ever read Celine?" I say.

"No."

"He was a doctor in World War I, and he came out of it with this condition where his eyes couldn't follow anything. Like he was a human camera and things would enter his line of vision and leave it. Anyway, there's this scene in *Death on the Installment Plan* where the narrator, who has this same problem, breaks down and wishes that everything would stop so he wouldn't have to watch people always leaving."

"Nice," Marty says.

"Yeah. He made it all up. His real life condition, that is. But that's how my head feels and I'm worried about it. Like I'm sort of waving hello and goodbye at my thoughts, but not grabbing them." I pause. "Plus the pain. I could live with being scatterbrained if it didn't hurt so much."

"Pain's supposed to go away though, right?"

"Supposed to be gone already," I say. "They don't know so much. Don't trust them."

"What else you worried about?"

"That's about it," I say. "I still feel a little bad complaining around you."

"Do I look that bad?" he says.

"You look pretty bad." I start to laugh. "I'm sorry," I say.

"Shut up," he says. "No more apologies. That's the new rule, OK?"

"OK."

"So what do I look like? I haven't wandered in front of too many mirrors the past couple of weeks, you know. How bad do I look?"

"Actually, you don't look bad. I mean, I can't see you, just the wraps and the Striker Frame." I roll over to get a better look. I usually don't look at Marty when we talk. It seems kind of unfair since he can't look at me. "You know what you look like? Remember the old Superman show? How when he was supposed to be flying, you could tell he was really strung up with wire?"

"Yeah."

"That's how you look, wrapped in gauze."

"That's pretty bad," he says. "If I was you, I'd feel guilty complaining around me, too." He pauses. "You know how he died?"

"Who?"

"George Reeves. The guy who played superman on TV."

"How?"

"Suicide. Jumped out a window."

"Really?"

"Yeah. I always thought that was one of the funniest things. Superman jumps out the window and then splat. Great image," he says.

"That's funny?" I say.

"I made that up. He shot himself in the chest, so, no, it's not funny. But, if he'd jumped out a window, that would have been funny."

"You up?" Marty says.

"Up," I say.

"Can I tell you something?"

"Of course."

"First of all I'm tired of this shit. You know how many times they've tried to put the skin back on my arms?"

"Two?"

"Three. One before you came. It's kind of hard to get too excited about Skippy's harvesting at this point, you know?"

"But," I say.

"I'm not done. There's a couple of things bothering me. One is that I don't want to go under that knife again." He's breathing hard and choppy.

"You don't have to talk," I say.

"I don't want you to get better," he says.

"What?"

"I don't want you to get better. Do you understand? I mean, part of me wants you walking out that door tomorrow, but part of me wants you stuck in here with me." He takes a deep breath. "Sorry."

"No apologies," I say. "Your rule."

"Do you understand?"

"I think so," I say. "I do have to leave, though. Not tomorrow, but sometime."

"I know," he says. He laughs quietly. "I'm just worried they'll put some guy in next to me who plays the clarinet all night or reads out loud from Scientology texts or something."

"They might," I say. "You never know."

"I've gotten kind of used to having you around."

It was a Harley Sportster . . . Black . . . Nice bike. I might get about three thousand on the insurance, which should help with the bills. I wonder if my student loans are still due. Probably. Money doesn't stop moving just because you do. My grandmother, dead three years now, still gets her social security checks. Something like $450 a month. That's what? Almost fourteen grand? Death's been very good to her. The dead laugh all night at the sitcoms. They're cleaning up.

Border Radio

When I was thirteen years old, my father killed a man in front of me. The man my father killed was, I'm pretty sure, a stranger to my father. The man my father killed got into an argument with my father over the price of a parts car in our yard. The man my father killed had a wife who'd said he'd answered an ad in the paper and had gone to look at a used car. My father was a state trooper. He said that the man never made it to our house to look at the car.

I have no idea where my father took the man he killed's car, but I do know he drove it away with work gloves on after he had gotten rid of the body. I have no idea where he took the body, either, but the man my father killed was never found, as far as I know. Other cops believed my father's story and no one ever asked my father about that man again. The last I saw of the man my father killed was when my father threw him in the back of his GMC pickup and drove out of our driveway and I stood there watching until he was a rusted red dot in the distance.

But to really tell you what happened that day, the part that stays with me anyway, I have to tell you about my grandfather.

Background

In 1935, at the height of the depression, my grandfather had men paying him twelve hundred dollars apiece to graft goat testicles into their own balls as an impotence treatment. A nation was out of work and men woke with no purpose day after day, with lint in their pockets and lint in their minds and nowhere to go and nothing to do. A Model A Ford cost $400, and my grandfather, the less than honorable Dr. Lionel Charles Camoin was getting men to pay him twelve hundred dollars to graft goat balls into their testicles.

Complications

Some of his patients thought it was a cure and claimed wildly successful results. I still have some of the ads he'd put in local newspapers and the like. Whether these were made up men, actual men who were paid shills, or sincere pleased patients is beyond me. But, even if some of the success was real, the majority of my grandfather's patients were left mutilated and broke.

Most lived and were left with the hollow remorse of a terrible financial decision, surgically-induced permanent impotence, and chronic survivable infections. More still developed violent, stubborn infections that raged through their swollen hot balls into the blood stream and killed them in a matter of a few horrifying, painful weeks.

According to newspapers my grandmother saved for their contentious divorce, thirty percent of the men who my grandfather operated on died. His hospital, which was really just a Connecticut barn with a dirt floor that grew mushrooms in the corners in dank soil, became a lightning rod of the media of the day. For a time, he was the biggest news story since the kidnapping and killing of the Lindberg baby.

The Potency of an Eighteen-Year-Old Man

My grandfather advertised on radio, in the papers, on flyers pinned to the newly planted telephone lines lining themselves like giant wooden exclamation signs all over the New England countryside.

He painted his impotence cure on road signs, on barn roofs and on the walls of his panel truck that he drove all over Connecticut and New York.

The procedure involved drilling out a hole in each testicle, which was then stuffed, like loading a musket, with goat testicles that had been ground into a paste of animal flesh. Picture, as my father once told me, a stuffed olive.

"It will bring you back to the potency of an eighteen year old male! Foster the power of youth and vitality with Dr. Camoin's miracle cure!"

License

The infections were, as I said, painful. Brutal. Balls swelled beyond the capacity for the sutures to hold and men's scrotums exploded in pain, puss, blood and various viscous fluids, escaping their heated, dying bodies.

Seventy percent of the men lived. The majority, perhaps pressured by the shame of exposing their impotence, and their desperate measures to cure it, kept their mouths shut. Enough of them raised enough hell, though, to pressure the state to pull my grandfather's medical license and he was run out of Connecticut, under the threat of jail on top of losing his job, all the way down to Mexico.

A New Country

My grandparents had, as I said, a terribly violent separation. My grandfather, before it was all over and while they were still married, had my grandmother committed to the Fairfield Hills Mental Hospital for hysteria. Husbands could do this to wives in 1935. Among her many unnecessary treatments, there was a series of electroshock therapy that left her unable to remember the beginning of her sentences by the time she reached the end of them. My grandfather, as a result of her diminished capacity, was awarded custody of my father.

Whatever chance my father had of growing up without turning into a beast died the day the judge gave him to my grandfather, who took him down to Mexico, where he had opened a new clinic. My grandmother rotted in her madness until, in an attempt to run away from the mental institution, she died of exposure in a ditch off the Merritt Parkway in 1947.

I'm descended from at least two generations of savage men and have lived my life clouded by a fear that what made them what they were flows through my veins and fires sick neurons in my head.

Fifty Thousand Watts

Mexico was perfect for my grandfather. He could still be a doctor, still bilk desperate men from their money and still raise his son, all while living the life of a very rich man in Mexico.

The down-side? While it was difficult to find men with twelve hundred dollars in Connecticut in 1935, it was near impossible in Mexico. So my grandfather bought a radio station. In 1935, the most power a United States radio station could use to broadcast was five thousand watts. In Mexico, there was no limit to the power of the station's wattage, and so my grandfather ran 12 hours a day of programming, all of it sponsored by his Wonder Clinic with its miracle cure for vitality and youth.

Fifty thousand watts was powerful enough to send his signal all the way to Canada. By 1938, my grandfather was broadcasting 24 hours a day, with some of the biggest stars of the era. The Carter Family sang for 2 hours a day. Jimmy Rodgers played until he was too tired to work—his tuberculosis brought blood from his lungs and killed him. A young Bob Hope did radio plays. All sponsored by my grandfather's revolutionary vitality clinic.

Fifty thousand watts obliterated all the radio programming in Texas. In Louisiana and Arkansas. My grandfather's station could be picked up by the most unlikely of antennas. It became a famous phenomenon of its time. Newspapers talked of radio signals coming from the barbed wire around farms, unseen ghosts of language emitted from water towers standing in lonely fields. Anyone with metal fillings could open their mouth and have the Carter Family singing songs of sin and redemption from their teeth.

In Athens, Ohio in 1938, a man was killed by his wife because she was convinced he'd been possessed by the devil when jazz music came from her mouth at night when he was asleep. She was acquitted.

My grandfather, too, was killed in 1938. But it wasn't by some crazed person who thought they were hearing the devil. It was by a very rational and angry man, deep in a fevered illness caused by my grandfather's surgery on the man's testicles. The man who killed my grandfather didn't live long enough to go to trial—he died from complications from my grandfather's miracle cure four days after shooting my grandfather.

Leveling the Playing Field

The United States Congress, acting quickly in response to domestic radio corporations who were having their shows bulldozed by unregulated border radio towers, allowed greater power for domestic stations. In the matter of a few years, the power was regulated just about everywhere and the days of a long distant signal bullying its way through the airwaves were pretty much over.

You still hear radio signals in wire fences and fillings, especially old mercury ones, but you have to be pretty close to a powerful tower—not half a country away.

My father and I were within sight of WADC's radio tower the morning my father killed that man.

The Man My Father Killed

But, it wasn't the Carter Family and it wasn't a song of sin or redemption coming from the dead man's mouth. My father and I had been chopping wood and loading a cord of it into his beat up old red GMC truck when the man my father killed came to look at the car. We'd had the truck radio on, the doors open, and we were listening as the Baltimore Orioles were taking a 3-1 lead in the World Series over the Pittsburgh Pirates.

The man and my father were talking about the parts car my father had for sale. It was a 1973 Mercury Cougar that my father had taken in trade for building a friend of his a bathroom. My father wanted two hundred dollars for the car. The man offered seventy-five.

Somehow, and staggeringly quickly, this became something to fight over and then something to kill over and my father, who was still holding the axe we were using to split the firewood, hit the man on the side of the head with the dull end of the axe.

I was, as I say, thirteen. I didn't know much about the world. But I could tell right away the man was dead. He fell at what looked like an impossible angle—his legs bending opposite the way they're supposed to for a minute before he collapsed on his back onto the woodpile. His head was smashed, with a cruel divot behind the left ear. On that side, his head looked like an apple with a crude bite out of it. The rest of him, though, looked good enough to sell you something on TV. His eyes weren't wide open and scared like in the movies, but kind of lazily looking off into the distance.

And his mouth was open, and he was picking up the World Series, too, just like the radio in the truck. My father paced. He lit a Marlboro cigarette and the cigarette smoke merged with the smell of wet leaves and the smell of damp soil and the smell of freshly split wood. My father paced some more and turned off the radio in the truck, and then stared down along with me at the man he'd killed. The radio was still coming from the man's mouth and we heard that the Pirates had lost and were down in the series three games to one, which made it all the more surprising when they pulled it off and won the series in seven games, becoming only the third team ever to come back and win after being down 3-1 in the World Series.

But at the time, no one thought they'd come back, and my father and I stared at the man my father had killed, his open mouth broadcasting the Pirates' highly improbable odds of victory.

Beano's Deal

"Why me?" Gray says again to Mellisa, the features editor.

"You know boxing, you know sign language," she says from behind her desk. "You're as close as we come to an expert on this one."

"OK," he says. "But a boxing ape?"

"Don't call him an ape. Word is they're sensitive about that."

"Who? His owners?"

"No," she says. "The apes." She looks flustered. "The chimps, I mean."

"A boxing chimp?"

"Retired," she says. "A retired boxing chimp. Here's his file," she says, handing over a manila envelope. "Read it. Get to know something about him. This could be a good, solid, human interest piece if you take it seriously."

"Human?"

"Just don't embarrass me."

He leaves the office and goes out for lunch with a file marked "Beano," in grease pencil on one side.

Gray has lunch with his friend Holly at the Hob Nob, an outdoor bar on 301. The bar's a reminder of the good days, before Interstate 75 carved its way through the West Coast, reducing the 301 strip to boarded-up memories of tourist money.

Now, Gray notices, not much is left. The old Sarasota Hotel is abandoned, except out front, where the old bar was, there's a labor pool. "Men Wanted. Every day. 5 AM."

"Maybe I should try that," Gray says to Holly.

"Five bucks an hour to snap your spine," she says, mocking a wince. "Stay where you are."

"It's driving me crazy," he says. "This isn't what I went to school for. Interviewing seventy-year-old widows and now . . ." Gray shakes his head and leaves his thought unspoken.

"Now you're talking to monkeys." She sips her beer. "Could be worse," she says, and points at the labor pool.

"I work at a fucking retirement magazine, Hol. And I'm not even in a good department."

"Christ, Gray. You're in Florida. During retirement season, you could walk from one end of this state to the other on the hoods of powder-blue Cadillacs." She dips her peel-and-eat shrimp into the cocktail sauce and chews. "Of course you work for an old folks' magazine. Know your demographics, pal."

Gray fingers the edge of Beano's file. The manila has dark blotches from droplets of sweat off his forehead. He shakes his head and opens the file. He looks across the road, up and down 301.

"God's waiting room," he says.

At one-thirty, Gray enters the weathered gate of Tyler's Museum for Performing Animals. In the sixties and seventies, the Tylers traveled the country—mostly the Southeast—with birds that jumped through hoops, trained gators, your run of the mill honking seals, but their chief attraction was the boxing chimps. Dan Tyler would offer $500 to anyone who could go three rounds with any of the animals.

The chimps were dressed in boxing trunks, given ten-ounce gloves and a muzzle over their jaw so they wouldn't use their teeth when the opponent was wounded. Beano was the last of the chimp boxing champions, retired in 1974 with a perfect 155-0 record. In twenty-two years, using six different chimps, "Dandy" Dan Tyler never once had to fork over the $500.

Gray checks all these facts one more time in his car before going into the complex to do the interview. Beano's the last of the chimps still alive. The rest of the animal retirement home is a sad affair. Mrs. Tyler runs the place, Dandy Dan has been dead for years, and it's a little run-down.

Some tropical birds dressed like humans are perched in outdoor cages. A small pool sits at the end of a weed-peppered brick path. The pool houses both the seals and the gators, with a chain-link fence separating them.

Gray is led to the back porch where he spots a chimp in an Adirondack chair, sipping a drink. The chimp is dressed in bright blue boxer shorts. His drink has an umbrella, he smokes a cigar and for some reason, Gray can't get the image of Joseph Cotton in *Citizen Kane* out of his mind. He puts the file down and introduces himself in sign.

"No need," Beano signs. "I read lips."

"Really?" Gray says. He sits down and opens his note-pad.

Beano rolls his eyes. "No, I lied," he says.

Gray has interviewed several impatient, surly old people in the past few months, but this encounter still has him a little off-balance. He decides to start simple and basic.

"So how old are you?" he says.

"Twenty-six," Beano says.

Gray smiles. "We're the same age," he says.

"Not exactly," Beano says.

"Why? How old are you in human years?"

"How the fuck should I know?" Beano snaps. His hands are quick. He talks fast. "How old are you in chimpanzee years?" He sips his drink and puts the glass down. "*Human* years," he says.

"Sorry," Gray says. He tries to get on Beano's good side, though he's beginning to wonder if one exists. "So how old am I in chimpanzee years?"

"Young," Beano says. "You're young, OK?"

"Fine," Gray says and opens the file. He's getting nowhere, but he's got to come up with something that resembles a feature or he could get canned. Too many old people have called Mellisa and reported Gray to be short-tempered, bumbling, incompetent. You name it. He knows more and more every day he's not well-suited for this gig, but he can't afford to lose it. He pushes on.

"Do you miss boxing?" he says.

Beano looks at him. "Do I miss this costume? Do I miss being a piece of meat? Being part of a freak show?" He shakes his head. "Next question."

Gray scribbles in his pad. "I'll take that as a no," he says as he writes.

"Look at me," Beano says. "I can't read your lips."

"I just said that I take it you don't miss it," Gray says.

"Bingo," he says. "I miss the violence, though. I miss beating up on humans."

"155 of them," Gray says.

"Something like that," Beano says.

"No losses."

"I had a jack-hammer jab."

"I had a nice left hook," Gray says.

"You box?"

"Golden Gloves," Gray says. "Not professional."

"What was your record?"

"I don't know," Gray says. "Thirty-something and four," though he knows it was exactly thirty and four.

"We should go at it," Beano says.

"Box?"

"No, dance. Of course box," Beano says. "Your attention span is shit, you know that?"

"I don't box anymore," Gray says. "Besides, I think you might be out of my league."

"You're right about that," Beano says.

By four, Gray figures he has enough information to do something that resembles a professional effort of journalism. He meets Holly at the Hob Nob.

"How'd it go?" she says.

"Not bad," Gray says. "I like him better than the people I've been interviewing lately."

"He's got a personality?"

"Shit yes," Gray says as he sips his beer.

Gray is at work at home, transcribing notes when the phone rings. He picks up the receiver, but there's no one on the line. He hangs up. It rings again.

"Hello?" Gray says. Nothing.

"Hello?"

There is a chimpanzee noise. *Eek, eek, eek.* And then a hang-up. It happens four more times in the next half-hour and then stops for the night.

At eight in the morning, the calls start again. Gray drives to Tyler's, after showering and filling up on coffee. Beano is out on the back porch again.

"You're calling me?" Gray says.

Beano nods. "I have a proposition," he says.

"How'd you get my number?"

"You're listed," Beano says. "Sit. We need to talk."

"About what? The story's almost done."

Beano shakes his head.

"What?"

"I want to box you for my contract," he says.

"Contract?"

"Mrs. Tyler needs money. She'll let me go for a thousand. We box. I beat you, I'm free. You beat me, I'm yours. Deal?"

"I don't have a thousand dollars," Gray says.

"Then help me break out."

"You're crazy," Gray says.

"Box me for it. Same deal. You win, it's the last you'll hear from me." Beano looks at Gray. "Come on kid. You think this is easy? I've never asked a human for help before."

"What would you do?" Gray says. "If you beat me?"

"When I beat you," Beano says.

"Whatever. What would you do?"

"That's my business," he says.

At eight, the phone calls start again and Gray realizes that Beano is not a chimp who takes no for an answer. Four times in an hour, Gray's phone rings, no noise at all on the other end, followed by a hang-up. At nine, the phone rings again.

"Look," Gray says into the receiver, "I'm thinking about it, OK? Leave me alone for a while and I'll talk to you tomorrow." He's not sure if Beano can understand words, but he thinks maybe his tone will get the message across.

He hangs up. The phone rings and he picks it up on the first tone.

"What do you know about freedom?" he demands. "It's not all it's cracked up to be."

"Gray?"

The voice on the other end throws Gray. He lights a cigarette and sits down, using an old Diet Coke can as an ashtray. When he ticks his ash, the tip of the cigarette fizzes in the liquid gathered at the lip. He re-lights the cigarette.

"Gray?"

"Yes?"

"Most people just say hello."

"Mellisa?"

"Yes." She pauses. "What's wrong with you, Gray?"

"I thought you were someone else," he says.

"I gathered," she says. "Who?"

"Beano."

"The ape?"

"Chimp," Gray corrects.

"You getting a lot of calls from lower mammals?"

Gray tells her what's been going on the last couple of days. He tells her about his meeting, the interview, and finally about Beano's deal.

"You're joking," she says.

"That's what he wants," Gray says.

"Meet me in the office at eight," she says. "No, nine. I'll see what I can do."

"Do?" Gray says. "What? Do?"

"Tomorrow," she says and hangs up.

Gray decides to go meet Holly for a drink at the Hob Nob. When he returns after midnight, there are ten messages on his machine. The first has chimp squawks on it. Beano sounds at once angry and desperate. The rest of the messages, Gray erases without listening to.

"Here's the deal," Gray tells Beano. It's ten in the morning and Gray has just come from a meeting with Mellisa and the editor-in-chief of *Sunset Years*. "You and I box."

"And you break me out," Beano says.

Gray shakes his head. "The magazine puts up the money."

"How do I get free then?"

"I don't follow you," Gray says.

"You win, the magazine owns me. I win, I stay here. What the hell kind of deal is that?"

"No," Gray says. "The magazine doesn't want you. They just want a story. Either way, you're free."

"Either way?"

"You can't lose."

Beano sips his drink. He looks at Gray. "Where will I go?" he says.

"I thought that was your business," Gray says.

"It was, but I didn't think it would get this far. Can I stay with you for a while?"

"You're joking."

"I'm not."

"I don't think so," Gray says.

"Just for a while," Beano says. "I could do some promotion work for the magazine. Appearances, things like that. Make some money and move out. We could be neighbors."

"I don't know," Gray says.

"Please," Beano signs. Over and over, his hands in a repeated gesture. "Please."

Mellisa loves the idea. The magazine has recouped their investment in Beano by selling tickets and advertising space. Any money made on the chimp beyond the fight is pure profit. Beano, she thinks, would make a great mascot for the magazine. The deal is struck. He will make appearances and have his own advice column for retirees, ghostwritten by Gray.

The fight is scheduled for three rounds. Gray steps into the ring in a bright red robe with "Nellie's Kosher New York Deli" emblazoned across the back. He is mildly hurt the advertising space on his back cost less than half that of Beano's.

Beano steps in the ring in neon blue trunks, his matching robe open. Beano is sponsored by "Quality Tires." The referee gives them instructions and gives the order to shake. Before heading to his corner, Beano winks at Gray.

It ends quickly. Gray's height, which he thought to be an advantage, turns out to hurt him. He protects his head and Beano goes wild on his torso. He thrashes Gray's rib cage with repeated right hooks. Gray is beaten like a gong for two minutes.

He drops his hands out of exhaustion. Beano spots the opening and lands one, two, three, jabs. One of them splits Gray's lip. He falls. The crowd sounds funny to Gray, their cheering seemingly underwater and muted. He sees his blood and snot on the canvas and passes out.

Holly comes to see him in the hospital. The doctors have told Gray he'll be fine. A couple of cracked ribs, three stitches, one on the inside, two on the outside of the lower lip.

"How you feeling?" she says.

"Been better," Gray says, though he's happy to be floating in a morphine haze. "How's Beano?"

Holly smiles. "Toast of the town. He's at Nellie's Deli today, some liquor store tomorrow. The old folks love him. They drive him around in a convertible," she says. "The Beanomobile."

Gray smiles and his lip hurts. "The Beanomobile?"

"Cute, huh?"

"Very. How's my apartment?"

"Fine," she says. "He cleaned up. He moves in next door to you in a month or so. When that weird guy's lease is up."

The Beanomobile is parked in Gray's space when he comes home from the hospital so he has to put his Subaru down on the street. The walk, less than a block, stings with each breath. Gray walks up the stairs. There's a barbecue on his porch, full of food. It sends smoke up under the awning, then into the sky.

Beano sits in a new lawn recliner, his feet up on the railing. He smokes a cigar, and wears a tailored gray suit.

As he comes up the stairs, Gray notices a woman taking Beano's picture and a man in a chair taking notes. The woman puts the camera on the table and talks to Beano in sign language, though Gray—at this distance—can't make out the words. Gray comes up to his balcony.

"How you feeling?" Beano says.

"OK," Gray says. "How you making out?"

"Fine, fine," Beano says. He smiles a wide chimpanzee grin and introduces, fingers flying, the reporter and the photographer to his roommate.

"This is Gray," he says. "A friend of mine."

Gray says hello, then walks past them to put his mail down on the table. Beano follows him in; the screen door bounces on its hinges.

"New suit?"

"Nice, no? Feel the fabric."

Gray holds the lapels between his index finger and thumb. He nods. "Nice," he says. He looks at the chimp. "Listen," Gray says. He takes a breath. "This has got to stop."

Beano begins to sign something, but Gray looks up at the ceiling fan in an effort not to be interrupted.

"No," Gray says. "This has got to stop. I've done all I can and I'm not sure I can do anymore for you. No more parking in my space, no more barbecues at my house with people I don't know, OK?"

Beano has looked down at the floor. Gray straightens the chimp's head and looks in his eyes. "OK?" he says again.

Beano nods. "I'll be done with these two in a while," he says. "Get some rest." He slaps Gray lightly on the cheek. "We'll take the top down. Go for a drive."

Gray guides the Cadillac down Gulf Road, over the International Waterway Bridge. He has to drive slowly to see both the road and Beano's hands but, he figures, what's one more slow Cadillac in Florida?

"I need one more favor," Beano says.

Gray pauses. He looks straight ahead. "What?"

Beano pokes him in the shoulder. "Teach me to drive," he says.

"Drive?"

"I have to get out of here."

Gray pulls the enormous car into a boat launching lot. He looks over at Beano.

"You all right?" Gray says.

"No," Beano says. "It's the same as always."

"What is?"

"The deal was, I beat you I go free." He shakes his head, looks out at the blue-green water of the Gulf. "I'm not free."

"Who is?"

"This isn't my world," Beano says. "Your world, not mine."

"What? You want to hop around in the forest?" Gray says. "Is that the deal?"

"No," Beano says sadly. "I couldn't do that. I'd die."

"Well, what then?" Gray says and looks over at Beano. The chimp stares at him, his face all frustration and angst. He doesn't say anything for a moment and Gray looks away. Beano punches the dash three times hard and the glove compartment flops open.

"Beano signs slowly, "It's the same as always." He repeats this sentence so many times that Gray's eyes adjust to the movements. His eyes plead for understanding.

After a while, Gray only catches the word "always," in the cycle of motion, like a beep on a tape loop. He looks straight ahead and, every couple of seconds, catches the word in his peripheral vision. *Always, always, always.*

"So," Gray says. "What now? You want those driving lessons?"

Beano slumps back in the big leather seat. His feet, Gray notices, don't quite reach the floorboard, they graze the carpet. "No," he says. "They'd catch me." Beano looks across the parking lot. He and Gray spot at the same time a group of people, mostly children, have come toward the car.

"Let's go," Beano says.

Gray slides the car into gear and heads out onto the Gulf road. Beano, perhaps, Gray thinks, out of habit, turns and waves to the crowd left standing in the lot.

Earthquake

It makes the cows, especially the blind one, crazy as all hell and it screws with the bank machines. You're at a bar in Arcata and the A's are playing the Giants on TV and the quake hits three hundred miles south. You see it, but you don't feel it. It fucks with Ricky Henderson a whole lot more than you. When you get home, drunk, you find out about the cows.

They're running all around the yard, smashing into the sides of the house and the dead 1974 Forest Green LTD that sits next to your Subaru in the gravel driveway. You are from the East. From a city. You didn't know cows could run. You never dreamed they could be frightening.

You made a mistake moving here—the earthquake has nothing to do with this, you were long gone before this hit—and you're moving the day after tomorrow.

You live at the dead end of a dirt road in McKinleyville, California. 1963 B avenue and you find it strange that the house sits in a town named after one assassinated president, and your address is the year of another's.

You live with Buzzard Wendell. You placed an ad and he answered it.

Buzzard Wendell, in his mid-forties, is wanted by the federal government, the California Parks Authority, the Audubon societies of three states, and both the local and the national Friends of Animals.

He fought in Viet Nam for three tours and lost his right leg, just below the knee joint—a career Marine who, after a series of nervous breakdowns, became an errand boy for Mrs. Kissinger before quitting the corps in the early '80s and starting his second career, which was hurting and killing animals protected by the US Government's Endangered Species Act.

Buzzard Wendell has a praying mantis earring, dipped in shellac for preservation. He has a Florida black panther tail on his Harley. A necklace made from the teeth of Oregon sea lions. His gear bag is an armadillo shell. His boots are alligator.

He comes to the house in oil-stained Levi's, a slight limp caused by his prosthetic, a "Loud Pipes Saves Lives" t-shirt, and a nine millimeter tucked into his wide brown belt at the small of his back.

Buzzard Wendell is a walking junkyard of death and he takes the room next to yours in the house.

You get home and you're pinned in your car. You open the door a couple of times, but a cow slams into your door and you stay inside. The back window of the LTD is smashed in. You think you might die. Killed by cows.

Buzzard drops all five of them—you didn't know there were five, until they're dead and still and the cold air steams around their wounds, there was no way they seemed so few in number, you would have guessed ten at least—and the world goes quiet.

"Thanks," you say to Buzzard as you head into the house. You are still drunk and this is the strangest night you've had in a while.

He shrugs. "They were suffering," he says.

The next day, you go down to the bank to get the rest of your money. You never close an account. This is what you do—you take money out down to the last twenty and leave the rest. You keep moving—you'll have money all over the country. The machines don't work. The earthquake knocked all the bank machines down. Your money is tied up in natural disasters and technology.

You move, eventually, back East. People ask you about earthquakes.

"They fuck with cows and they screw up bank machines," you tell them.

"Really?" they say. "Bank machines?"

Whatever Happened to Billy Brody?

.

People stare.

Billy Brody gets this a lot, more often since *E! Entertainment* did that special on child stars of the '70s. There was Brody, sandwiched between Dana Plato and Danny Bonaduci, coming across as better off than the dead Plato and less well off than the Malibu-d, funny, working, but still fucked-up Bonaducci. The show touched on most of Brody's major transgressions—the parents stealing the money, the drug arrests, the rehab and the repeat and fade of loss and pissed away second and third and forth and so on chances. A loser, pretty much, was the portrait. Which was fair, Brody suspected. He didn't mind so much being portrayed as a loser, though he did get annoyed as hell at being presented as a cliché.

You know the story: kid actor, talented or not, does a few commercials, lands a role as a precocious wisecracking kid on some lame sitcom, in Brody's case the three-season *All By Myself*, about a divorced dad who hooks up with a waitress with a wisecracking son (who talked like the kind of adult who gets his ass kicked in the real world), show gets axed, parents steal whatever money wasn't bled off by the various handlers, managers and agents, and you only hear about the kid in the ex-celebrity police blotter until he dies or finds some sort of focus in his life.

At the moment, though, no one's staring as Brody and Wendell Craig are riding in the Granny Wagon, which is what Wendell calls the big sky blue Pontiac Safari 6000 wagon his grandmother gave him when she had her legs amputated from diabetes. They're on their way from Los Angeles to Twenty-nine Palms to buy some Percodan from some guy Wendell barely knows out in the high desert.

Wendell's behind the wheel. Brody's hopped over the front seat into the back, trying to find the Buck Owens tape that's fallen under the seat. The blue carpet's stained a rusty brown in the shape of Florida and smells of stale coffee, surf wax and diet coke. Brody bends down, turns his head to the side, and slips his hand under the seat. He feels the tape and sweeps it out, along with a blue lozenge and three pills.

Brody hops the seat, slides in the Buck Owens. The tape player clicks in, and Buck starts singing about heartbreak and loss—voice as pretty as a coyote at night, lonely as a good idea in this world. Brody holds out the three pills in his left hand and tries to flick off the beach sand and blue carpet hairs.

Brody says, "What are these?"

"You got them off the floor?" Wendell says.

Brody nods.

"Then they're garbage, dude."

"I got the Buck Owens off the floor. That wasn't garbage."

"I just dropped the Buck Owens. God knows how long those have been down there."

"Could they be pain pills?"

Wendell shrugs. "Maybe. But probably not."

Brody considers them. The three pills are the same. Buck sings about the girl he left back in Japan, halfway around the world but forever lodged like a sliver in his sad heart. Brody pops two pills in his mouth and they rasp down his throat. He washes them down with the bottom of his ice coffee. Coffee grounds stick to his tongue and teeth and he works them out, spitting.

Brody puts the last pill on the dashboard. "If they're any good, that one's yours."

"Generous with my drugs," Wendell says.

"You said they were garbage," Brody says. "Guinea pig gets two." He sees a late-'60s muscle car pulled to the side of the road with its hood up. Steam farts out into the smoggy hot air.

Forty minutes later, Brody is suffering. The Granny Wagon slugs up the hills of Highway 60 and Wendell's turned off the air-condition to avoid overheating, but the car's not responding, and he has to turn on the heat. The drugs have started to kick in, and Brody remembers having felt this way before. He groans.

Brody points to the pill sitting in the dust of the dash. "You don't want that pill, dog."

"Good to know," Wendell says.

Brody shakes a groggy head and the world oozes by his open window. When he talks, it's like blowing a hair dryer into a dry mouth. "Tuinal," he says.

Wendell shakes his head. "Sorry, man. Pamela must have left them."

Brody wants to puke. Wants to fast-forward his life six or eight hours until this is over. Tuinal makes you gooey stupid. Your brain slogs like a heavy wet bar rag and your organs feel like caramel apples, all hot, sticky and wet. Picture all the hair in the world stuck with gum and you've got Tuinal.

Brody thinks about trying to sleep it off before they get to Twenty-nine Palms, but there's not enough time. They're less than an hour away as he sees the windmills outside Palm Springs spinning dully in the heat and Wendell turns off the freeway onto Route 62 and heads northeast toward Twenty-nine Palms.

A half an hour later. Coffee at a Sizzler in Yucca Valley. From the melting heat of the car to the walk-in cooler of a desert restaurant. Wendell's going over the game plan. Brody's still sticky in the Tuinal. Shivering with wet cold. Punch drunk. Slow on the uptake. Not the sharpest tool and all that.

All he wants, needs when you break it down to its essentials, is some pain pills for the fucked up neck he got surfing last winter and has let go, not sought proper care, because his Screen Actors Guild medical lapsed after the commercial strike made work as scarce as joy at a Brody family reunion, if such a thing were ever to occur. This, the need for the Percodan, is not a lapse in his re-hab, he tells himself, but an absolutely necessary medication that any responsible doctor would have prescribed, had Brody left the resources to see such a doctor. He needs to be pain free so that he can work full days and hustle some money for this film idea he has.

"I don't know this Arley Hopper so well," Wendell says.

Arley Hopper is the drug dealer. The desert rat with the chemical lab. "What are you saying?"

"There could be some trouble?"

"How much trouble?" Brody says.

Wendell shrugs, looks at his coffee before sipping. He puts it down. "Enough to mention it as a potential snag beforehand."

Brody nods, considers. "What are we prepared to do about this trouble?"

Wendell laughs. "We run."

One of the things that Brody likes and respects about Wendell is the fact that Wendell doesn't, won't, carry a pistol on a drug deal. They would do what they needed to do, and nobody had to get hurt.

"How you feeling?" Wendell says.

"Like flypaper," Brody says. "Like shit in a port-o-let."

Wendell looks at his watch and says with a fresh breeze of friendly apology and concern, "We can't wait any longer." Wendell's trying to be kind.

Brody looks around the Sizzler lunch crowd. People buzz around him and Brody watches them like they're distant cousins on the food chain. A few notice him and he can tell from experience, they want to come up and talk to him, recognizing him from their television past—he's their walking nostalgia from some long-cancelled show. They stare. He may as well be in a petting zoo.

Wendell says, "When we hit Twenty-nine Palms, go to Al's Swinger Bar off Adobe Road and call a cab."

"We can't drive to his place?"

They get up. Wendell drops three bucks as a tip. "His drugs, his rules," Wendell says.

Brody nods, knowing, having learned long ago, that scoring is one area where the customer is always at the disadvantage.

They drive through Joshua Tree, past the Joshua Tree Inn, where Gram Parsons overdosed, back in 1973. Morphine and alcohol. The words alone make Brody salivate. As overdoses go, that had to be a relatively painless one. Floating on a cloud out of the world.

Ten miles south of them, in the National Park, is where the park rangers found what was left of Parsons' body at Cap Rock after his road manager stole the body from LAX and torched it in the Park in an attempt to honor Parsons' wishes to be cremated at Joshua Tree. Some fans wrote on Cap Rock, made it a sad memorial place.

Brody's been at the memorial sight, fucked a woman named Maryanne once at Cap Rock. She was a major GP fan. Brody had met her at a beach party in San Onofre, and they drove drunk out to the desert in a convertible that lacked a reverse gear. They went into the park. It was a cold night, and she was still wearing beach clothes—cut off jeans, no underwear and some paisley cotton top. She lit a candle, put on a CD of "We'll Sweep Out the Ashes" set it to *repeat* and told Brody to fuck her from behind and not talk so she could imagine it was Gram Parsons fucking her. She told Brody this. The desert was bright from the full moon and it looked like day-for-night shooting. They drove back, one headlight off at a three-o-clock angle, in the quiet pre-dawn, drove back to the beach where Brody got into his Toyota and never saw her again.

Whenever Brody comes out to the desert, he thinks about those connected scraps—Gram Parsons alone, slipping away at twenty-six in a rented bed of a motel room. Two people fucking on a rock, Maryanne pining for a dead man she never met, Brody pining for something else he's yet, in 36 years, to find a name for.

He's thinking back, taking stock. A life full of misplaced desire. The smell of burning wax in the air and whisky on a beautiful woman's breath and the cold clean high desert wind. People who meet once. People entering and leaving each other's lives. A life full of scattered moments and fragments, of evidence and event piled up behind him. Is that what adds up to a life? All these people, and all the nonsense we did with and to each other, he thinks. You follow it, study it, maybe it leads somewhere, maybe it tells you something, like the debris field around an accident. Like the charred ruins the insurance investigators poke through and make a story out of.

Brody tries to cheer himself up. "Are we there yet?" he singsongs like a kid.

Wendell says, "Close. We get the cab. We meet the man out by the airstrip. Francis Road." Wendell turns up the heat and Brody feels like he'll pass out. "If we hit the airstrip, we went one road too far."

Just outside of town, Wendell uses his cell phone to call for the cab. "Al's Swinger" is a club off Adobe Road that's been boarded up for a while. They pull in and wait. In less than ten minutes, a beat up K-Car slumps and bounces into the lot.

Their cab driver is a woman whose teeth are going every direction except the ones you'd expect from teeth. It's like she swallowed an M-80. They get in the back and she drives them out of town and into Wonder Valley.

Francis Road is one of a thousand dirt roads beyond downtown Twenty-nine Palms. It comes after roads with names like Cactus Jack and White Sands and, Brody's favorite, Thunder Road, which makes him think of Robert Mitchum, the greatest thing, along with the Wiffle Ball, to ever come out of Bridgeport, Connecticut, where Brody was born.

The cab slows with the hard right turn, squishes down into the sand and spins wheels for a second before catching and jerking up the road. She turns into the first house on the left, lets them out, and pulls away.

The house is white, with a rolled out roof and a large screen porch. Fascia board has warped and pulled itself off the frame of the house like they'd had a disagreement. The pump house lacks a door and the stucco's been shot-gunned down to its chicken wire guts.

The water heater's been left exposed to the elements—an old electric Sears 600 model, white with faded gold script lettering. There are a series of vehicles in the yard—a 74 Duster on blocks, a Vista Cruiser wagon and a Jeep pickup with a thousand gallon water tank trailer hitched to it.

Brody stops, looks out at Wonder Valley. Heat waves belly dance on his horizon. The Tuinal flip-flops in chest. His head aches. He doesn't know if he can go through with this, wonders if it's too late to call it off. To get back to LA, go to bed and wake tomorrow with the promise of America and a new start. But sometimes pulling back is the wrong thing, like braking in an ice storm slide—sometime the logic is backwards. Accelerate, head down, steer through, and you'll be fine. Brody walks toward the house.

Two men meet them before Brody and Wendell get to the porch to knock. There's a man in his '40s, with a Wild Turkey baseball cap, and a younger guy in his late teens, wearing a white t-shirt and Levi's. The kid's twitchy, reminds Brody of a small dog, but he's skinny as a parched corn stalk and he avoids eye contact and seems to be scared of Brody and Wendell and so registers to Brody as not much of a threat.

Wendell sticks his hand out to the older guy, who must be Arley Hopper. "We talked on the phone."

The older guy takes Wendell's hand. "We did. Pleasure doing business."

"Same," Wendell says and introduces Brody. Wendell points to the kid. "This your partner?"

Hopper smiles, amused. He says, "Just another satisfied customer." He lights a cigarette. "Where's your car?"

Wendell says, "Where you told me to leave it."

"Good. We'll take my car back to yours, then we'll head out to my office."

They switch out Arley Hopper's Vista Cruiser for the Granny Wagon at Al's Swinger, and head back in the direction they came. They pass Hopper's house, and drive further out, Hopper riding shotgun to Wendell's driving, Brody and the kid in the back. Brody stares at Hopper, who looks so serious he's comical. Big, imposing and goofy all at once, like an Easter Island stone.

The Granny Wagon heaves past the airport, past this small pinky-finger of a bar called "the Mouse Trap" where it looks like you'd be lucky to get five people drinking at once. It looks like a trick bar, like there'd be a contest to see how many clowns or frat boys you could shoehorn in there. It reminds Brody of Shriners and their cartoon small cars, all grabbing one for the road at a dinky bar. The kid's looking at Brody, up-and-downing his profile. Brody knows this look, this feeling.

"Don't I know you?" the kid says.

"I don't think so," Brody says.

"You were on that show," the kid says.

Hopper turns around, gives Brody the once over.

The kid says, "What the fuck was that show called?"

Brody gives in, says, "*All By Myself.*"

"That's it," the kid says. He hops on the seat a couple times, slaps his thighs, excited. "Shit, man, wait till I tell Brenda. I met Bobby Brody."

Brody thinks about correcting the kid, but lets it go.

The kid says, "Arley is hooking me up with Viagra. We worked together at the speedway. And Arley can get me speed and Viagra. How 'bout you guys?"

Brody sees Hopper wince a bit at the kid being so open. He's right to be worried—if the kid lives in town, he'll crack like a ripe guava the minute he gets pressured to give up names.

"We're getting something else," Brody says. Then it hits him. "How old are you?"

"Nineteen," the kid says.

"You sick or something?" Brody says. "No offense, but what's with the Viagra?"

"I don't *need* it. Me and Brenda, we split one, and then we go all night."

"Good for you," Brody says.

"Or when I wrestle," the kid says.

"You wrestle Brenda?"

"No, dude. On the team. At school."

The conversation's draining what little energy Brody has and he doesn't say anything. He looks out at all the jackrabbit homesteader shacks—little structures built after World War II by desperate men, drawn by the promise of five free acres of government land, so long as they built a shack to code. Thousands of people built here, but few stayed. There are over sixty-five thousand of them, some as small as eighty square feet, abandoned in the Mojave, most of them in Wonder Valley and Landers.

"I'm a hell of a wrestler," the kid says. "I can beat anyone, so long as he's not Samoan."

Brody looks at him. "You can't beat Samoans?"

"They have very thick skulls. And they tend to head-butt."

"That's ridiculous."

"You don't wrestle, dude."

Brody starts to argue, but lets it go, as Wendell takes a hard turn onto another sandy road.

When they get out of the car, Brody talks over the car to Arley Hopper. "You know anything about the thickness of Samoan skulls?"

"They're thicker, from what I hear."

"You just hear that in this car?"

"No," Hopper says. "It's something I've heard prior to this."

"Really?" Brody says.

The shack's beat to hell, but it's locked up—plywood door held up with two carbon locks. Around the side are several fifty-five gallon garbage cans. This, the cans, the locked door, is the clear sign to not fuck with the place. But, the cops won't do anything because half of the labs are abandoned and booby-trapped. Nobody wants anything to do with people like Arley Hopper and this realization smacks Brody as he follows him toward the shack. In the yard are a rusted '60s Ford pick-up, a couple of mattress frames and some old fabric and magazines and books.

Hopper says, "I need you guys to take off anything that could throw sparks."

Brody knows the drill. Sparks mean fire and fire mixed with phenylacetic acid is trouble. It's highly flammable. Sunlight off of a mirror can light it, and it's colorless and odorless and it burns the linings of your lungs and you're dead before you can cry for help.

The kid starts into the shack. Hopper sticks out an arm to his chest and says, "What the fuck did I just say?"

The kid looks at him and doesn't say anything. Brody and Wendell hold back. Brody feels and hears hot wind blow his hair and heat his neck.

Hopper points at the kid's belt buckle. "Take it off. And dump any lighters or anything flammable outside." He turns to Wendell and Brody. "You guys, too."

Brody's wearing tan work boots with scars of paint all over them from art department work he's done when the acting jobs thin out. The work boots have metal eyelets for the laces. "These?" he says.

"Off," Hopper says, in a calm voice.

"This is stupid," the kid says, taking off his belt.

Hopper pushes him against a plywood-covered window, and wraps his meaty hand around the kid's throat. The kid's making gurgly noises. Gasping.

Hopper says, "I would rather strangle you to death right now than have your dumb ass risk my life or business." He relaxes the grip. "We're clear?"

Wendell says, "Everybody OK here?" He pauses. "We're just doing business, right? Nobody needs to get hurt."

This settles Hopper a little. The kid's a mess, but an obedient one, so Brody figures there might not be any more trouble. He plops his shoes down on the magazines and looks at one of the sun-worn books at his feet. *DIAL-A-FORTUNE: How to Make a Fortune in Phones.* Next to it is a bunch of fabric. A broken sewing machine. This was somebody's house. A life. He wonders when they pulled up and left. And why everything's here. The heat on the concrete slab is coming through his socks and it feels good.

Brody's the last one in the shack. There's not much to it—it's one room, maybe four hundred square feet. There are two deep sinks, gravity-fed from the roof tank, and a bunch of empty pills caps of several sizes and shapes. And there's a safe underneath one of the deep sinks.

"You," Hopper says to the kid, "were in the market for Viagra." He opens the safe and counts out ten pills, holding them out toward the kid. "Sixty bucks"

The kid takes out a fat roll that has at least two, Brody sees, hundred dollar bills on the outside. It's a roll that announces *I'm stupid* to the world as loud as a ship's horn. The kid gives over the three twenties and says, "You got any G?"

"You see a fridge here?"

"No," the kid says. "How about E? I heard you could make that from Sudafed."

Hopper laughs. Points to the kid and says to Brody and Wendell, "Look at Mr. Science, here. Gonna put me out of business."

"Do you have any?"

"No," Hopper says.

The kid points to some milky yellowish crystals that Brody recognizes as meth.

"How much for some of that?"

Hopper looks hard at him. "Scoot. Let us do our business, and we'll meet you when we're done."

The kid heads out of the shack. Brody sees him swipe some of the meth.

Hopper doesn't seem to notice. "Shouldn't do business with kids, but that's where the money is." He chuckles. "Them and the Marines. Those boys love the speed."

Brody says, "That's comforting. We're being protected by armed speed freaks."

"Better than being invaded by them," Hopper says.

"Good point," Wendell says.

Brody hears a rustle of metal outside. Hopper doesn't seem spooked, so Brody ignores it, guessing that he knows best here. Hopper says, "So how many can I get you?"

Brody wants, needs, two hundred, but it's not what he can afford and hears Wendell say, "Fifty Percs."

He nods and starts into the safe. He fiddles around in there for a moment before taking a Ziploc out with the pills, which he gives to Wendell. Brody get flat and depressed when he realizes that twenty five percodans won't keep him buzzed for even a day.

There's a scratching at the plywood door, like a dog trying to get in, then a flopping sound, along with a high wheeze. The three men dart out of the house to find the kid on the concrete slab in front of the house. He's sucking for air, his chest heaving up and down, arms at his side, as he thrashes around. Brody goes down to help him, and right off gets a wallop of the kid smelling like stale urine and ammonia. It burns in Brody's throat right off. The kid hits Brody in the face as he seems to be trying to scream, and Brody is thrown down against a 4-inch plumbing vent that someone had left in the slab when they were still planning a life out here. His eye strings right off.

Brody starts to roll toward the kid, but he doesn't make it. Hopper grabs Brody like a fumble and runs him off the slab. Brody feels the concrete change to sand as he's dragged away, the sand sticking to his sweaty back.

Hopper says, "Get away and stay away." He's still holding Brody's collar.

Brody rolls over and looks at the kid. Wendell is by the front door of the shack. Hopper tells him, too, to stay away from the kid, whose pleading, confused eyes are focused on Brody for a moment, and then elsewhere. Brody sees the kid drop a pipe. The kid flops around, fish on a deck, desperation and need literalized, made flesh, the sound like that cat-puke noise, and then a thin wheeze, and then nothing.

Wendell stands over him, open-mouthed.

Hopper walks behind the house. Brody stands, looks over the kid, who's clearly dead. Brody's never seen a dead person before. He's seen people overdose, but they've always made it. The kid's eyes are leaving no doubt. They're dry and dusty looking. Dulled already, but still filled with the confusion that he fixed on Brody a moment before. Brody sees the kid's belt, still neatly snaked by the front door where he left it.

Hopper comes back from behind the house. Brody can see where the kid lit up, over one of the cooking drums. Hopper's shaking his head as he walks back. "The stupid fuck."

"Are we safe?" Wendell says.

"Not with a dead kid on the porch, we're not."

"I mean are we safe from whatever killed him?"

Hopper says, "So long as you don't light a flame over a drum of phenylacetic acid, you are." He looks at the kid. "This is fucked up. We are in it deep here, boys."

It comes to Brody in a snap that he thought things were bad this morning, but that things can always get worse. That the crap you were complaining about yesterday is what you'll die to defend today. It comes to him fast. He's sorry for the stupid kid, but he's not going to jail for this. This is a situation that needs a remedy that allows for Billy Brody to live his life.

Brody looks at Wendell. "You have a gas can in that car?"

"Why?"

"Do you?"

"No," Wendell says.

Brody goes into the shack, leaving Wendell and Hopper behind. Brody unscrews the longest of the flex-pipes from beneath the deep sink and comes out to the heat and moves over to the car. "Get him over here."

"Is he safe?" Wendell says.

Hopper looks confused. "Sure, he's safe now."

"You want to burn him?" Wendell says.

Brody says, "What I want has nothing to do with this. He's nothing but evidence now. He needs to be gone."

Brody thinks for a moment, wanting to come up with a better idea, searching for it like lost keys, and not finding it.

Hopper grabs the kid beneath his armpits and drags him over to the car. The kid's Levis catch on an ocotillo. Brody goes over to help and gives an extra tug and feels his neck twinge. The kid's leg snaps free and Brody gets him over to the car. Brody starts siphoning out the gas. It comes, and he spits the beginning of the flow on the kid's open eyes.

Brody smells and tastes the gas, which mixes with his sweat in the desert heat. Hopper drags the kid's body under the hose, so that he's wet, head to toe. Brody crimps the hose.

Hopper nods. "Back inside?"

Brody nods, says to Wendell, "Help me, here."

Wendell's in a daze, looking like the zombies in *Night of the Living Dead*, he stumbles over straight-legged and grim-faced and helps Brody carry the kid inside. When they get inside, Hopper's already there, lifting his safe. They drop the kid in the middle of the room. Brody stands back, his neck aching. Hopper drops his safe, goes into the kid's pockets and digs out his wallet and keys. He takes rings off his fingers and puts it all in his shirt pocket. They step out of the shack.

"This is so fucked up," Wendell says.

Brody nods. Hopper says, "The kid fucked up. We were just do-ing business." He goes back over to the car and gets the hose Brody used for the gas. He lights it, and throws it into the shack. The three of them move away as the floor lights up, and then the kid, whose boots Brody can see from the door.

"We need to get out of here before the cooking drums go up," Hopper says.

They get into the Granny Wagon as black smoke, like from a tire burning, starts seeping out and up from behind the plywood windows. The windows of the car are down. There's a crackling high-pitched brittle noise, along with the low whoosh and hum of the gas flame that sounds like a base amplifier's feedback. They pull away, Brody in the backseat, watching the smoke in the rear-view mirror.

"Will anyone say anything?" Wendell says.

"We were never here," Hopper says. "Just another shack. Some kids burned it down. Happens all the time."

Brody wants to believe this. Wants this, like so many things, to have not happened. Regret is not a strong enough word for what he's feeling now. He keeps seeing the kid's eyes, keeps thinking of some mom and dad sitting down to dinner, wondering where their kid is. Thinking about Brenda, who will now tell people for the rest of her life about her dead high-school sweetheart. None of this is his fault, he tries to tell himself, but still, it's a sucker punch of a day and he feels like hell. Ambushed. Damaged.

They drive without speaking back toward Al's Swinger Bar. Wendell slides Buck Owens back in the tape deck and Buck starts singing about the streets of Bakersfield. Brody tries to focus on the words and melody, tries to lock into something familiar and beautiful. They turn onto Highway 62 and head toward Hopper's car and the tires thump the blacktop under Buck and the Buckaroo's rhythm. When they get to Al's Swinger, Hopper drops half the kid's money on the seat as Brody gets out of the back and into the front.

"I don't want that money," Wendell says.

"Fair's fair," Hopper says. "I didn't intend on taking the boy's money." He bends down and looks into the car. "It's probably best if we don't do business again."

They're back on Highway 62, and Brody, not knowing what else to do, is counting their half of the kid's money. There's two hundred and ten.

"I wonder how that kid came to have four bills on him," Wendell says.

"Beats me," Brody says. The money flaps in his hand. "Let's go to Vegas," he says.

"Vegas?"

"For better or worse, this is found money. Let's see if we can do something with it."

Wendell shakes his head. "What the hell?" he says. "Why not?"

Outside of Baker, home of the world's tallest thermometer at the Bun Boy restaurant, Wendell asks Brody what time it is. Brody checks his watch. His arm is oily with sweat and he still smells like gasoline.

"4:30," he says.

"How hot do you figure it is? Over 100?"

"Easily," Brody says. "I'd say 110, maybe 115."

"No way," Wendell says. "I'll bet it's no higher than 104."

Brody's stayed in Baker, has shot low-budget movies out there twice in the summer, when rental fees are cheaper. He knows that in the summer, it seldom reads below one-ten. "No way it's under 110."

"It's a bet."

Ten minutes later, they come up on Baker on the I-15, the sun burning the back of Brody's arm and neck, and the world's tallest thermometer reads 114.

"I win," Brody says, but they never agreed to an amount, and they don't talk anymore about the bet, or anything else for a while. Wendell pulls the Granny Wagon into the gas station and fills it up. Brody goes inside and buys a couple of bottles of cold water and a Diet Coke. They get back on the I-15 and Brody pops two more of the Percodans and waits for his neck pain to ease. He feels his eye, swollen and raw from where he hit it on the plumbing vent. Wendell puts in *Exile on Main Street* and clicks ahead, turning the stereo up when "Stop Breakin' Down" comes on. Brody closes his eyes and feels the car sweeping toward Las Vegas, toward the Golden Gate, where you can still play dollar table blackjack and turn a couple hundred bucks into something that might make a difference in your life.

A Headache from Barstow to Salt Lake

Clarence "Box" Templeton was a two weight class Marine boxing champion during an amateur career that spanned from the start of the Korean War to one year after when, in 1954, he turned pro and had a more-or less-good five year run that included a night at the old Felt Forum where, in a loss on points, he rattled Archie Moore with body shots so hard and strong that "The Mongoose" ("You feel it when a rib goes," Box once told Coleman. "It's hard and then it's soft.") told reporters he couldn't sleep right for a month.

"Watch out for that boy," Moore said back in 1955. "Learn to spell his name. He's here to stay."

But Box Templeton was not there to stay. A year after the Moore fight, he'd become nothing more than a side of beef club boxer, propped up and pieced together enough by Wednesdays to be beaten on Fridays for fifty dollars a fight.

He married Coleman's Aunt El in 1958, and ended up at the Long Beach shipyards. There may have been a decent piece of him left—Coleman has always thought there must have been for El to take him in—but by the time Coleman arrived in 1970 after his parents died in a car wreck, all that was left of Box was hatred and scar tissue. A head more full of lumps, stitches and revenge than ideas, El once said. So when El fell in love with Mavis Clemont—who taught fifth grade math at Coleman's school—he knew where his loyalties fell and he never said a word to Box. When El and

Box moved to the desert, Mavis sent Coleman her letters, and he'd hand deliver them to El, so Box wouldn't open her mail and find out. When El died, Mavis sent letters to Coleman. "Men ruined our lives," she wrote in the last one. "And we let them."

Billy Pritchard, who Uncle Box says is dumb enough to think that the driver's test is hard and mean enough to drink shooters of rattlesnake poison and grow an inch each time, is at the front door to Box's bar when Coleman pulls up. Get the money and get out is what Coleman's thinking. The ground crunches, hard and dusty, under Coleman's feet and he wonders, as he does every time he comes to visit, how anything or anyone can live on, in or on top of all this. The earth, sucked dry, split, puckered and cracked—like El's bloody knuckles, flaky as pastries, the year before she died— spits up plants short as tongue depressors with root structures so stubborn thick and expansive that even a creature like Billy Pritchard couldn't yank them up.

"You're here," Billy says.

Coleman looks up and squints; heat waves quiver and spasm off the metal roof. He sees the sign with the typo above the door—the sign they never changed that reads *Trucker Welcome*, left from the Chinese couple El bought the place from when she and Box packed it up, called it quits and left the rat race when Box's lungs started to bleed and the shipyard gave him the early retirement, wished him well on his way to healing or death—whichever he might find— out in the desert.

He walks towards and into the bar, brushing by Billy. "I am here," he says. "Where's Box?"

Billy grabs Coleman, turns him around. "What do you do?" he says. "For him. What do you do?"

Coleman lights a cigarette, wishes he was inside with a beer. *Coldest taps in the desert,* that's what El told him when she bought the place. Coleman looks at Billy Pritchard, then at Billy's hand still on Coleman's arm—the hand with the gouge from the meat- packing plant—the hand that's not really a hand anymore.

"Box?" Coleman says.

Billy releases his grip, shakes his head. He points inside. "His business why he thinks you're worth two shits."

"He doesn't," Coleman says.

"So you know?" Billy says.

"Know what?"

Billy looks surprised—like he's a kid caught shoplifting. He looks out at the desert. "You better talk to Box."

Uncle Box has big, dry, cool hands that swallow yours whole the way snakes and their hinged jaws take in rodents. Box gives you a handshake, it's like you're in some prehistoric petting zoo and touching something that was dead before your kind were born. The palms still glow silver from the years at the shipyards—the same metal fragments that make the hand glisten are the chips and fragments that sent his lungs over the edge and made them drown in their own blood. Once a week, someone—first El, and now Billy—takes Box to the hospital to get his system flushed and his lungs and liver checked out. He looks up from his wheelchair at Coleman.

"Why did you come?" Box says and snorts.

"You asked," Coleman says. He turns to the entrance to the bar and sees Billy Pritchard looking as if he's waiting for someone.

Box talks like he's got permanent phlegm in his throat. Most times, he snorts and swallows. When he's drunk, he gets lazy and spits blood clots into a beer glass. By the end of the night, the clots, oily, purple and dense, settle at the bottom and the spit floats on top so the beer glass looks like a Lava Lamp when it's shut off. Little air bubbles cling to the clots. You watch it long enough, and one'll release and climb its way through the spit to the surface.

"You came for her money," Box says.

"She left it to me," Coleman says.

"True," Box says. "She did."

A car pulls up and Billy Pritchard and a thin man Coleman has never seen come into the bar.

"You know Billy," Box says and nods. "This is Tommy Nova. He's been helping out."

The thin man shakes Coleman's hand. "My real name's Tommy Davis, but everybody calls me Nova because I drive a Nova." He motions toward the parking lot. He looks at Box. "We'll shoot some stick. You'll tell us?"

Box looks hard at him. "I will."

They walk to the pool table at the back of the bar. "Tommy Nova's gonna kick your ass," Tommy says to Billy.

"Come back to the office," Box says.

He spins his chair and wheels ahead of Coleman into the office.

"Here's the deal," Box says. He drops an envelope on the table that separates them. "Ten grand in there and it's yours. But I know what you did to get it."

"I didn't do anything," Coleman says.

"You lied." He snorts and swallows. "She lied to me. And you lied for her, Coleman. And now I know. And someone's got to pay for those lies."

"Wait," Coleman says.

"Shut up!" Box says. "In a perfect world, I should kick your ass bloody for this. But I'm not the man I was, so Billy and Tommy Nova will do it for me. One beating for your lies, and one for hers."

"You know," Coleman says. "How?"

"How is not important and it's none of your goddamn business," Box says. He takes a couple of deep breaths and snorts. "What you need to know is that justice must be divvied out." He holds his hands apart. "And with El gone, you're what's left."

Coleman shakes his head. "Keep the money," he says and gets up.

"Don't run," Box says. "If you run, they'll kill you." Box takes a sip of his drink. "And the money's yours. Those were El's wishes and I intend to carry them out."

Coleman looks at him.

Box smiles and coughs. "Those boys are loyal to me. Dumb, but loyal. The way you were to your aunt. It's a good quality—you just put your money on a loser." He shakes his head. "Don't run. I don't want you dead."

Box picks up the office phone and punches line two. He calls a number and Coleman hears the phone ring out in the bar and sees line one light up on Box's phone.

"This is my Kingdom," Box says into the phone. "And my enemies shall burn." He hangs up the phone and looks at Coleman. "I got that from her. From one of her books. Never forgot it."

Billy Pritchard starts it with a right hook to the stomach that makes Coleman drop to his knees, throw up and heave for air. Tommy Nova kicks him in the ribs and Coleman hears one or two of them give—hard and the soft, just like Box said. Coleman collapses and rolls on his side in his puke. He feels his bladder release and his piss spread in a pool around him. After Tommy Nova's kick, there's no way to tell who does what. The world alternates between bright colors and blacks and, every once in a while, Coleman catches blurry sight of Box sitting above him.

Coleman wakes up in a chair in front of Uncle Box. Billy Pritchard and Tommy Nova are drinking at the bar. Box gives Coleman a beer and a glass of water.

"That one was yours," he says. "You'll have a headache from Barstow to Salt Lake and you'll piss blood, but you'll heal. That's for lying to me. You understand?"

Coleman fades in and out. Each breath stings. "Understand," he says.

"You did wrong," Box says. "Admit it. Say it."

Coleman looks down at the ground and sees his blood splattered on the wood. He did the right thing, he's sure. Wrong to Box is not wrong in general. But he's where he is, and there's only one answer.

"I did wrong." He holds his head in his hands, elbows at his knees. A couple more drops of blood fall on the floor and it looks to Coleman like a Rorschach test. *What do you make of this?* it says. *What do see here?* And you give your answers, knowing there's no single right one, but there are any number of wrong ones.

Uncle Box wheels up close to him. "You'll live" he says. "The next one is for El, understand?"

"I understand," Coleman says.

Billy Pritchard and Tommy Nova come over to Coleman.

"Go easier," Box says. "Give him the beating she would have had. This is hers."

They nod. Coleman looks down and spits out a chunk of his cheek. *What do you see here?* the blood says. *What do you make of this?* This one is El's and he can take this for her. Maybe this one can have a reason that works for him, he thinks, as Tommy and Billy lift him from the chair and knock him to the floor again.

Do Not Concern Yourself
With Things Lee Nading Has Left Out

How Hank Collins ends up on this desert freeway—he has to admit it, a desperate and defeated man who will, from this day forward, be mugged and gnawed by guilt every morning and forever before he even tastes his coffee and faces whatever sorrows that day will bring—how Hank ends up shooting straight-arrow through burned out sage brush and over the flat and lifeless tarmac with a bag full of baby rattlesnakes bundled and angry on his Chevy's passenger seat, how Hank ends up here, in this moment, is the story of the story of how Hank left Geri ten years after common sense and everyone with a brain in their head had told him to scoot, head for the hills, vamoose and get on with the shambles he'd made of his life.

This begins yesterday at *Tosker's Tavern* outside of Bakersfield, with Hank's Uncle Cleeve—the lawyer in the family, the man known for his ability to tap dance through minefields of obscure legal technicalities to keep society's ugliest and worst out to roam and menace, the man nobody trusts and everyone, at one time or another, needs. Hank has needed him more than most and this time, with Geri in for tire-ironing a highway patrolman, it's serious.

Cleeve takes a sip of his beer. "Nothing I can do, Hank."

Hank runs his fingers over the brass rail of the bar. There's a basketball game on the TV. The Running Rebels are playing one of the pasty-white Utah teams.

Cleeve thumps his runty knuckles on the bar and signals for another. "This ain't D&D, boy. She left that young man out there for the coyotes. Lucky he ain't dead." He shakes his head. "This is real time and you, me and The Good Lord don't change that."

Cleeve isn't religious—*The Good Lord* is Cleeve's name for money and has been for as long as Hank can remember. Cleeve hired Hank a few years back to make a sign for behind his desk—*Me & The Good Lord Will Set You Free.* Hank mounted, as ordered, two freeze-dried Diamondback rattlesnakes, coiled and eating their tails on either side of the words.

Cleeve's big on rattlesnakes—he goes to the roundup every year and enters himself in the snake toss. He acts like a big man about it, but it's silly and dumb—those rattlers have been in garbage cans for a month before the roundup and they've been starved and burnt out in the sun to the point that they might as well be worms. Cleeve and his buddies toss back and forth acting like it's the most dangerous thing in the world.

Hank, just once, would like to see what they'd do with a fair fight—how tough Cleeve and his boys would be with an angry young nest that keeps striking long after their target is dead. A nest of babies could puff Cleeve up green and bloated like the devil's Michelin Man.

Hank pictures him there, under the *Me & The Good Lord Will Set You Free* sign, his cowboy boots, polished and pointy with angles like a geometry text, leather and silver on his desk.

"The trooper's alive," Hank says.

"Who went to law school? Who's got the diploma, boy? Is it you?"

"No. It isn't me, Cleeve."

The bartender puts a mug in front of Cleeve, who nods his thanks. "But you're sitting there telling me my business, is that it?"

Hank has been here before. "I was just making a point."

"Fuck your point," Cleeve says. "Your point has no point." He starts counting on his fingers. "One, she's driving on a suspended. Two, she drops a state trooper out in the fucking desert—which is frowned upon, whether he lives or not, you pissant. Three, she's got serious mental deficiencies—which I can list for you. You want that?"

"I'm aware of her situation," Hank says. He's holding back here, while he sees himself splitting Cleeve's head open with a pool cue. *Cleeve is necessary*, he tells himself. *You need him.* "I married her, remember?"

"Boy, Grief shook your hand ten years ago and you asked her to move in," Cleeve says. "You were a fool and it's time to move on."

Fact is, Hank's finally getting around to quitting Geri and he has no idea how to go about it, which leads him to Melissa Garvey, who trains dogs for the blind and who, two years back took Geri in and, six months ago, dumped her back in Hank's lap.

Hank gets out of the car and walks over to where she's putting a Shepherd through some remedial paces. Hank shifts his weight for a minute and lights a cigarette.

Melissa sees him and stops. "Hank."

"Pretty dog," he says.

"They all are." The dog seems interested in Hank and makes a slow friendly move toward him. Melissa gently pulls on its harness. "Why are you here?"

"You heard about Geri?"

"I did," she says.

"Cleeve says it's bad this time." He takes a drag of his cigarette, sees the dog sniffing toward a pigeon with a bad leg. Melissa tugs on the harness and the bird walks away, looking like a kid on a scooter.

"That still doesn't explain why you're here," Melissa says.

"You love her," Hank says.

"Loved," she says.

Hank shrugs. "Thought you'd want to know."

"Like you just heard, I already knew." She bends down and pats the dog on the head. "And since you're still here, interrupting me and my work, I figure you got something else to say."

"You don't like me," he says.

"That ain't news, either," Melissa says.

"You know how they say when people are looking for advice, they go to someone who'll tell them what they want to hear?" He's about to crush his cigarette with his heel, thinks better of it and pinches it out with his fingers and drops the butt in his shirt pocket.

Hank says, "I'm thinking of leaving." She doesn't say anything. "I'm looking at my life in ten years, and I don't see it being different." He feels stupid, like all limbs are prosthetics he just got and doesn't know what to do with. Clumsy and stumpy and dumb as a brick.

For the first time since he came on her property, Melissa doesn't look like she wants to run him off. "She won't change."

He shakes his head. "Get worse, from what they say."

She bends down, checks something in the dog's ear. She stands up. "Take off, Hank. Make yourself a life."

He stands there a moment. Melissa bends back down toward the dog.

"Thanks," Hank says.

"You still hunting snakes?" Melissa says, but doesn't look up.

"I don't like it, but I need the money."

"No excuse," she says. "What'd they ever do to you?"

"Nothing. Except put money in my wallet."

"Don't think because I told you to leave that I think you deserve anything other than what you've got. Geri's crazy, but that doesn't make you good." She looks up at him. "I still think you're a lousy person, Hank."

Hank lights another cigarette and thinks he may, after all, have come to the person who told him what he needed to hear. To Cleeve, Hank's a moron. To Hollis and Church, he's a victim of crazy Geri, and to the rest of the town, he's become the nice martyred husband. He watches Melissa with the dog, feeling, she's got it right; nailed him flush and hard and pure and straight as a 22-ounce hammer on a perfect swing.

"There's people that could give you an argument about that," he says. "About me."

"They'd be wrong."

Hank, not willing or able to argue, walks back to his car.

Grief, Hank thinks. A word to Cleeve, the man of words, ruler in the world of words, the man who does his shuck and jive with all the words he can find. Grief. Cleeve's name for Geri. *You gonna visit Grief, boy? You want me to bail Grief out and drop her in your Lay-Z-Boy? Grief runs out on you and you beg to get her back, boy.* Hank's heard it all over ten years and it plays like a tape loop as he drives. *Ten years, and all you've got to show for it is Grief.*

But, Hanks thinks, there's a world beyond Cleeve's little corner of the world, beyond his words. Look in Geri's eyes, and there's more than words there. It's hasn't been pretty, but Hank wants to tell Cleeve, it's bigger than you and it's bigger than me and she sees shit that would swallow you and your diplomas and your money whole, and she's lived through it.

Hank's been catching rattlers since the accident that knocked him out of the painting business four years ago. At the time, he was working for Dwight "Fletch" Fletcher, a former merchant marine who died in the same accident that smashed Hank's collarbone and separated both of his shoulders. And the reason, the reason Fletch is dead and Dewey Thomas wanders around town with a split melon for a head and brains is, in part, because Dewey was a lazy son of a bitch who hated Fletch and didn't change the oil in the company van when he was told to do just that.

Cause and effect, boy is how Cleeve told the story, gave it words and shape and how he got Hank a settlement. Dewey didn't change, hell, never even checked the oil, and the block froze up and Herman at the garage has to give Fletch a loaner van. A loaner van that's missing all but the driver's seat and so Hank blows down the freeway with Fletch next to him and Dewey behind him sitting in folding chairs that are bolted down to nothing. A retread tire goes, and so does the van and when it rolls, all that's left is the shell of that van with Hank turned upside-down. Paint is everywhere. Fletch's dog, Marty, is slit in half and next to Hank, and Hank can't tell how much of the blood is his and how much is the dog's. There is an organ, maybe, Hank thinks, a liver, but he's not sure then or now—warm, separate from Marty and next to Hank's head.

Fletch is dead, twenty, maybe thirty feet from the van and busted and bent backwards and into himself, crushed and squat like an aluminum can. There's no sign of Dewey. The highway patrol find him out in the desert an hour later ten miles away from the scene, his head open, just running a straight line away from the accident. He'd been running, they guessed later, from the minute he'd pulled himself up after the accident and Hank still marvels that—with how little of him was left in that head—there was something that told him to run and there was something that made him able to do it.

You'd never know to look at Dewey Thomas now that he'd done that run. He moves slowly and can't take three steps before he starts wiggling and shaking. He stops walking and starts shaking, looking like he's about to explode, and then it stops and he takes another two or three steps and it starts again. The doctors figure it didn't help him, that run he took. The accident fucked with his head and cut his brain, but by the time the patrol found him, the heat from the sun had blistered the exposed part of the brain and there was even less left of Dewey than there'd been when the van flipped.

But, it was Dewey's fault and Fletch's liability—or at least it was when Cleeve finished. The settlement, from Fletch's wife, was enough to cover most of the money Hank owed Cleeve for, over the years, keeping Geri at home and not locked up.

"Talked with the DA, boy," Cleeve says from behind his desk. "No leniency this time. Lock up or loony bin until the meek inherit the earth or she dies—whichever comes first. I stuck out my neck. I tried best I could."

Hank nods, knowing that Cleeve stuck out his neck for the last time two or three times ago. He's lying—they both know it—he hasn't done a thing this time around to help her.

"No arguments? No 'it's not her fault? She can't help herself'?" Cleeve takes a sip of his coffee. "She's gone. Forever." He leans forward. "You're following this?"

"I am." Hank looks up at Cleeve's *Me & the Good Lord Will Set You Free* sign and realizes that he's about to be free—from Geri and the life and people he's known for the last ten years. He feels strange. Dangerous. Foreign to whatever he'd thought of as Hank Collins up to a minute ago. He thinks about killing Cleeve and dropping the body near one of the gassed snake hollows.

Cleeve's secretary—and latest fiancée—Jennifer comes into the office and refills Cleeve's coffee mug. He looks at her, and says to Hank, without looking away from her, "What do you think of the new tits, boy?"

Hank raises his eyebrows.

"Wedding present," Cleeve says. "Straighten up, girl. Give him a good look."

"Dirty man," she says and pecks him on the cheek. He smiles, and Jennifer takes a runway model walk—hipswing, heel outside of the pinkie toe—out of the room.

After she closes the door, Cleeve leans toward Hank. "This dirty old man can lift seventy-five pounds with his dick. What can you do?"

"How the fuck would I know?" Hank says. Cleeve's obsessed with his dick—once a month, he gets Hank to kill a big rattler, as long and fat as a man's arm, and he has Jennifer slice the tail and Cleeve sucks the blood from the snake for five minutes. He says it's some Malaysian aphrodisiac, which it may or may not be—Hank hasn't bothered to check.

"You'd know if you took care of yourself." Cleeve points toward the door. "That girl appreciates that. She honors me. If I told her to put two more tits right under the two I bought, she'd ask how big." He points to his temple, then flaps a hand over his chest. "That's love, boy. Something you never understood."

"You feel safe, Cleeve?" Hank lights a cigarette. "In this office? At this moment?"

"What the hell kind of question is that?"

"What makes you think—when you wake up—that you're going to make it through your day?" Hank says. "Faith?"

"Money," Cleeve says. He looks up at the ceiling and yawns. "Guns."

"Same as faith," Hank says.

"They're not. Faith is a sucker bet. Those clowns reading the old testament, dancing with the snakes and doing the funky chicken on a bed of scorpions—that's faith." Cleeve takes a drink of his coffee. "What's into you boy?"

Hank shrugs, losing interest. "Feeling like I'm about to hurt someone." He stands up. "Thought it might be you."

Cleeve looks at him and doesn't say anything. Hank knows there's a 22 under the middle desk drawer—Hank routed out the gun notch himself—and that Cleeve's probably leaning toward it. If there's a time to do this, now isn't it.

Hank walks toward the door. "Thanks for everything you did for Geri."

Two ways, Hank thinks, you know you've lived in one place too long:

Everybody that has the slightest inkling to fuck you has given you at least one try.

When you know crazy people's secrets.

He knows some of Geri's, but that doesn't count so much because they've been together a while and she talks crazy night and day whether someone's there or not. Billy Mann is another case, though. Billy's been locked up for three years and, while everybody in town knows he's crazy—which he didn't exactly hide, you eat your own shit and spit it at a judge, among other things, you get a one-way ticket—only Hank Collins knows the reason why.

Hank walks in with a dozen roses for Geri and sees Billy near the admittance desk. What brought Billy to where he stands—ten feet in front of Hank at the mental hospital—started the night

Clyde, Billy's big brother and Hank's drinking buddy, brought home a graduated cylinder full of mercury from Mel's Pharmacy. Clyde worked at Mel's before he went into the army and—before he got caught and fired and arrested—supplied Hank with Valium and, while they could still be had, Quaaludes. This is years ago. Clyde's dead now—shot robbing a gas station in Ely during a heat wave two summers ago. Clyde probably went crazy too, but Billy got it worse, and he's here because his dead brother Clyde was an absolute idiot.

There was a party the night Clyde stole the mercury from Mel's Pharmacy. Things got ugly and stupid and Clyde ends up pouring the mercury into his hand and throwing it at the wall. Amazing stuff, it splats against the wall, and ends up in perfect balls all over the floor. He does this for a while, Clyde does—pours it in his hand, throws it at the wall. Clyde gets it in his head he should clean it up and he uses their dishtowels to soak it up. The shit was everywhere—in corners, rolling under furniture—and there was enough of it, Hank learned later, to poison a high school.

It wasn't long before Billy showed signs. Within a year, Billy's teeth were dropping out, flapping down off bloody and pocked gums. He made his own teeth for a while—filed down rocks and plugged them in with Krazy-Glue. With mercury poisoning, your short-term memory goes to shit—you black out, forget where you're standing, who you are.

Hank could and should have said something. He knows that much. But at the time, Clyde was still hooking him up with pills and there would have been all sorts of questions about how that much mercury ended up in that house. Questions with answers that pointed toward the drugs drying up, toward jail, and they were questions Hank didn't want in his life, so he kept his mouth shut and left the doctors to wonder what the hell had happened to Billy Mann.

Billy, before they finally put him away, became obsessed with what he called his "leaking." By this, he meant piss, shit and blood, or anything else that came out of his body. He drank his piss, ate his shit. Billy got cut in a bar fight once and, after he'd had his ass kicked from one side of Tosker's to the other, he spent half an hour on his hands and knees lapping his own blood off the floor.

Hank looks at Billy, who's got a vacant look in his eye. His tongue rotted to senseless meat a few years ago, and now Billy carries this little notepad and writes in it whenever he wants to say something.

"Billy," Hank says.

Billy stands there for a moment. He scribbles a note and hands it to Hank. Hank looks at the note which reads *Billy*.

"Billy," Hank says and looks at him, into eyes that don't seem to catch on or hold the world. He walks toward Geri's room.

Hank has no idea what state Geri'll be in when he sees her. The last time she was locked up, some clown mixed her on Aldolmet and Haldol and she was deep and ugly in psychosis and paranoid rage. He walks in the room. Geri's in her bed, propped up with pillows and a TV tray in front of her.

"Hey," he says. "Brought these for you." He holds out the roses and Geri looks out the window. He drops them on the TV tray and stands back.

"You always look so refreshed," she says without looking at him. "Like you've just come from a life."

Maybe semi-lucid, Hank thinks. Not all there, but not all gone, either. "We've got to talk."

"Why ostrich?" Geri says.

Hank shakes his head and pulls up a chair. He tries to make eye contact—bobs his head around like he's shadow-boxing. "Geri?"

"If lost, relax. Lee Nading says."

"Lee Nading?" Hank says, and finally makes eye contact.

"Lee Nading was an enormous man. A giant. A survivalist. Don't you know anything?" Geri looks at Hank. She seems to think this is important—like she's telling him something he needs to know. "Lee Nading says to relax. Conserve strength by moving as little as possible. Prepare emergency signals."

"Geri," Hank says. "Geri, I'm leaving." It doesn't seem to register. "I won't be back. Do you understand?"

"Lee Nading says relax," she says and smiles.

Hank feels himself sink and cave—this gets worse every time. He wonders if there's a way to get through to Geri, or what used to be Geri, and he wonders if maybe a better person than him might stick it out and find some answers.

Geri says, "Lee Nading says move as little as possible. Don't travel if confused."

Hank takes a breath. He's tried to say what he came to say, and she's not having it. *Play along,* he tells himself. Sometimes it works—you stay with Geri's train of thought, and switch tracks on her. "I'd never go anywhere," he says.

She looks up. "Is the sun receding? If the sun recedes you can drink your urine until it stops." Geri looks back at Hank and then up again. Hank looks at the ceiling, watches the cracks and the cobwebs for a moment. "You have two days if you don't move and the sun doesn't recede," Geri says.

"What if it recedes and comes back?" Hank says.

Geri looks at him again like it means something—like her words will change his world. "Lee Nading has only written about receding. Do not concern yourself with things Lee Nading has left out."

He reaches out to her shoulders and she slinks away. "They'll take care of you," Hank says. Geri looks out the window. "Understand?" She rocks back and forth and starts making a low humming noise. "Geri?" Hank says.

She hums louder and rocks slowly.

Hank slides the chair back and watches Geri. *This is it,* he thinks. A life filled with Billys and Geris and lumpy Dewey Thompsons sleepwalking through the world. All the words we've said to each other add up to this. This is what you'll see when you think of her. This is how you left her. Hank looks down the road, six months, a year, five years, and see his days lined up scowling and menacing and all the same forever. This is your life, Hank Collins. It's led to the woman you love locked away and talking nonsense for the rest of her life, to Dewey and his shakes and fits and Billy and his tongue as useless as a monkey wrench in his mouth and you were a part of all of it.

Hank watches her, studies her for a few minutes. He'll brand this image into him until it hurts more than it already does. He rocks back and forth with her motions. He starts to hum and hits her pitch and volume. Geri doesn't seem to notice. After a few more minutes, when he's done all he can to remember this, he walks out.

And after that? After that, Hank hits the desert and gathers the baby snakes. He flushes every hollow and nest with gas. When the snakes come out, he lops the heads off the adults. The babies, he dumps in a burlap bag on his front seat and he hits the freeway and pushes the Chevy hard and tries to decide what to do next. Like he's following his life instead of leading it, Hanks sees that he's less than five minutes from Cleeve's office.

Hank, as he sees it, is down to two choices:

One, he pulls off to the side of the road and opens the bag and lets whatever happens happen. Hank knows snakes—knows the odds are they'll come shooting out of the bag and pounce him. This isn't about faith, and it isn't about destiny or some other word as hollow as all Geri's and Cleeve's put together. There's at least twenty snakes in the bag and Hank knows what they're liable to do if he lets them out.

Two, he takes the car to Cleeve's office and dumps the snakes out there and leaves them for Cleeve in the morning. He'll strut in early, plop behind his desk with his feet up and he'll be dead before he knows it. He might get one or two before they converge, but a man doesn't walk into an office ready for twenty.

The car rumbles and shoots straight-arrow through burned out sage brush and over the tarmac. Hank's hands smell like gasoline from the snake hunt. This isn't, Hank decides, justice and it's not revenge. He doesn't know what it is, but it's as stubborn and it's as real as what sits next to him and it's going to happen that Uncle Cleeve, with his guns and his money and his words, will be, for once, without an argument.

Hank sees Cleeve's office in the distance. The car slows. Hank, still weighing the options, puts a hand on the bag and feels the alternating slip and coil of motion and stillness.

Biographical Note

Rob Roberge is the author of the novels *More Than They Could Chew* (Perennial, Dark Alley/Harper Collins, February 2005) and *Drive* (Hollyridge Press, 2006). He teaches writing at the Antioch University Los Angeles, MFA in Creative Writing, UC-Riverside's Palm Desert MFA program and the UCLA Extension Writers' Program, where he received the Outstanding Instructor Award in Creative Writing in 2003. His stories have been featured in *ZYZZYVA, Chelsea, Other Voices, Alaska Quarterly Review,* and the *Ten Writers Worth Knowing Issue of The Literary Review.* Non-fiction has appearing in, among others, *The Nervous Breakdown* and *Penthouse.* His work has also been anthologized in *Another City* (City Lights, 2001), *It's All Good* (Manic D Press, 2004) *SANTI: Lives of the Modern Saints* (Black Arrow Press, 2007) and *Orange County Noir* (Akaschic, 2010). He plays guitar and sings with several LA bands, including punk pioneers The Urinals. In his spare time, he restores and rebuilds vintage amplifiers and quack medical devices. For news and more info, visit & or email at www.robroberge.com